CROWN
OF
DREAMS

PENDRAGON LEGACY

≈ BOOK 3 ≈

CROWN
OF
DREAMS

KATHERINE ROBERTS

templar

A TEMPLAR BOOK

First published in the UK in 2013 by Templar Publishing,
This paperback edition published in 2013 by Templar
Publishing, an imprint of The Templar Company Limited,
Deepdene Lodge, Deepdene Avenue,
Dorking, Surrey, RH5 4AT, UK
www.templarco.co.uk

Copyright © 2013 by Katherine Roberts
Cover illustration by Scott Altmann

1 3 5 7 9 10 8 6 4 2

ISBN 978-1-84877-787-3

Printed and bound in Great Britain by CPI Group (UK)
Ltd, Croydon, CR0 4YY

For my father

Contents

Characters

ALBA – Rhianna's mist horse, a white mare from Avalon.

ARIANRHOD – Rhianna's maid, ex-maid of Morgan Le Fay. Her cheek bears a scar in the shape of a pentacle.

CAI – young squire at Camelot who becomes Rhianna's champion.

CHIEF CYNRIC – leader of the Saxons.

ELPHIN – Prince of Avalon and only son of Lord Avallach.

EVENSTAR – Elphin's mist horse, a white stallion from Avalon.

GARETH – older squire, Cai's rival.

KING ARTHUR – king of Britain. His ghost appears to Rhianna while his body sleeps in Avalon awaiting rebirth.

LADY ISABEL – lady in charge of the damsels
    at Camelot.

LORD AVALLACH – Lord of Avalon and
    Elphin's father. Leader of the Wild
    Hunt.

MERLIN – King Arthur's druid. Morgan Le
    Fay drowned his man's body but his
    spirit lives in the body of a merlin
    falcon. He can still work magic.

MORDRED – Rhianna's cousin and rival for
    the throne; the son of Morgan Le Fay.

MORGAN LE FAY – Mordred's mother, and
    Arthur's sister, a witch. Now dead, her
    spirit advises Mordred from Annwn.

NIMUE – the Lady of the Lake, who took
    King Arthur's sword Excalibur after
    Arthur's death and gave it to Rhianna.

QUEEN GUINEVERE – Rhianna's mother.

RHIANNA PENDRAGON – daughter of King
    Arthur, raised in Avalon.

SANDY – Cai's pony, rescued from the Saxons.

SIR AGRAVAINE – grumpy older knight.

SIR BEDIVERE – a young knight, also known as
    'Soft Hands' because of his gentle
    nature.

SIR BORS – leader of King Arthur's knights.

SIR LANCELOT – Arthur's champion knight,
    whose love for Queen Guinevere
    caused him to break the Lance of
    Truth when he fought against his king.

THE SHADRAKE – a dragon from Annwn,
    breathes ice instead of fire and hunts
    between worlds.

UTHER PENDRAGON – father of King Arthur
    and Morgan Le Fay. Now dead, his
    spirit lives in Annwn.

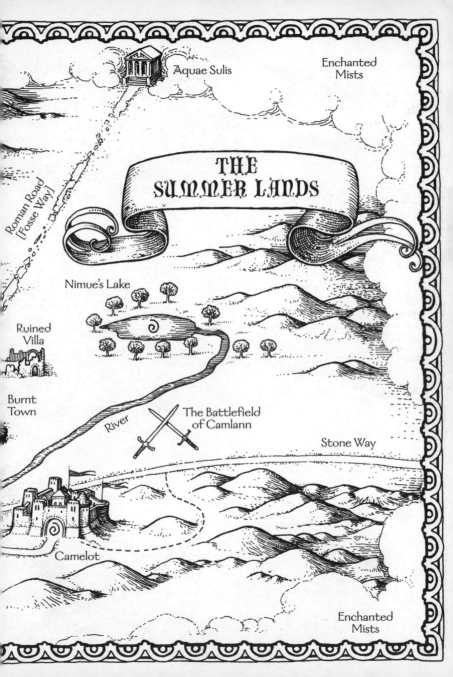

Four lights stand against the dark:
The Sword Excalibur that was
forged in Avalon,
The Lance of Truth made by the
hands of men,
The Crown of Dreams, which hides
the jewel of Annwn,
And the Grail said to hold all the
stars in heaven.

THE DRAGON'S LAIR

Mordred reined in his horse and eyed the cave behind the waterfall. A strange green glow came out of it, lighting up the valley. Water dripped from the trees, from his cloak and off the end of his nose. Why did dragons have to make their lairs in a land where it rained all the time?

"So what are you waiting for?" he snapped. "This must be it. Go in there and bring me King Arthur's crown."

His bloodbeards looked at each other uneasily. Seeing Mordred clench his fist, their captain drew his sword and rode reluctantly towards the wall of green water. His horse rolled its eyes and dug in its hooves.

"I think the horses can smell the dr-dragon, Master," he stammered.

"Nonsense!" Mordred said. "The shadrake's forgotten we were supposed to be following it. You all saw it fly off. If it had stuck around, we might have found this godforsaken place sooner."

"Horses sense more than men, Master," the captain pointed out, glancing nervously at the sky.

"Go in on foot, then!" Mordred used his good leg to kick the bloodbeard off his horse. "You can still run if you need to, unlike me. We'll wait out here in case the shadrake comes back."

The captain shuddered. But he knew

better than to argue with his master. Gripping his sword, he vanished into the hillside. Shortly afterwards they heard a muffled yell, followed by the rattle of falling debris. The water glittered eerily green, spooking the horses again. The men paled and crossed themselves.

"Oh, for Annwn's sake!" Mordred snapped. "Do I have to do everything myself? Leave your horses out here and follow me."

His stallion snorted at the water, but stopped playing up when Mordred growled at it. He ducked over the horse's neck to avoid the spray. Its hooves echoed inside the rocky tunnel, which sloped downwards and burrowed deep into the hillside. At every turn, the eerie green glow brightened.

Sweat bathed Mordred as he remembered

his underground sickbed, where he'd almost died after his uncle, Arthur Pendragon, wounded him with Excalibur during their final battle. But that had been a whole year ago. King Arthur was dead. The Sword of Light was in the hands of Arthur's daughter, who was afraid to blood the blade in case it stopped her taking the sword back to Avalon, where it would help bring her father back to life. Mordred had no such worries. As soon as he got hold of his uncle's crown, he'd ride to Camelot and blood his blade as many times as was necessary to claim the throne.

They emerged in a vast cavern, which stank of dragon. Jewelled daggers, rusty swords and dented shields were piled around the walls, along with what looked suspiciously like human bones. One of the piles had avalanched, and his bloodbeard captain lay groaning underneath it. His men hurried over to help.

"Leave him," Mordred snapped, seeing that the man was still breathing. "Find the crown, you fools! Quickly, before the shadrake comes back."

While his men searched through the dragon's hoard, Mordred rode his horse slowly around the cavern, prodding at the treasure with his spear. "Where is it, Mother?" he whispered.

"Here, my son," whispered a woman's voice from the shadows.

Mordred froze. His mother's spirit lived in the underworld of Annwn now, and until today he'd always needed her dark mirror to speak to her. "Where?" he said warily.

"Right under your feet, you foolish boy," the witch hissed. "What do you think is making the light in here?"

Mordred's horse stopped dead and threw up its head, banging him on the nose. He looked down and sucked in his breath.

His mother's body lay half buried under the treasure, her dress torn and stained. A crown encircled her dark hair, glittering with coloured jewels. As his horse's hooves dislodged the pile, he saw that one of these – a large green stone at her forehead – was glowing eerily. There wasn't a mark on her, and for a wild moment he thought she wasn't dead.

Then he saw her spirit rippling in the green light. *Dark magic.*

His gaze fastened greedily on the crown.

He slid clumsily out of his saddle and fell
to his knees beside her. He tugged at her
dress with his left hand, pushing the dragon's
treasure off her body with the stump of his
right wrist. "Help me, then!" he yelled at his
bloodbeards.

They came running.

"Morgan Le Fay!" the captain breathed,
still looking a bit dazed. "So this is where she
ended up. I always wondered how she died."

"That dragon must've killed her," said one
of the others, looking nervously at the tunnel
behind them.

"Don't be stupid," Mordred snapped.
"My mother's a powerful enchantress.
She controlled the shadrake. It led us here,
didn't it?"

Before his bloodbeards could point

out that the creature had abandoned them halfway to Dragonland, he reached for the crown. It was stuck, so he had to brace his good leg against the rock and pull. The crown came free with a sudden jerk, leaving a line of charred blisters across his mother's forehead, and rolled across the cave.

Mordred scrambled after it, picked it up and examined it carefully. Some of the jewels were missing, but it was definitely the same crown his Uncle Arthur had worn in their final battle. Triumph filled him. He ran a finger over the dent his axe had made when he'd split the king's helmet from his head, and smiled at the memory.

"Behold the Crown of Dreams!" he announced, showing it to his men. "You see before you one of the four ancient Lights, with more power than Excalibur, and twice as much magic as that useless Lance my cousin stupidly gave to her squire friend! This crown belonged to my Uncle Arthur and gave him the power to command men and dragons, and now it's *mine*..." He lifted the glowing circlet above his head.

"Careful, my son!" said his mother in a tone that sent a chill down his spine. "Don't put it on yet."

Mordred scowled as his triumph evaporated. "Why not? I thought that was the whole idea. I've got Pendragon blood, so it won't harm me."

"I've got Pendragon blood too, foolish boy, and it *killed* me."

He lowered the crown and glanced uneasily at his mother's body, which had begun to blacken and shrivel. "How?" he whispered. "How did it kill you?"

"I was careless. There's a jewel missing. I assumed it was a minor one, knocked out during the battle. But it's one of the magic stones, the one Arthur stored his secrets inside when he sat on the throne of Camelot. You've got to find that jewel and destroy it before the Crown of Dreams will accept you as the next Pendragon."

Mordred looked at the piles of treasure in despair. Find a single jewel among this lot? Worse, what if the stupid dragon had lost the stone on its way here, carrying the crown from the battlefield? It could be lying at the bottom of the Summer Sea.

"We'll be searching all year!"

"No you won't," the witch said. "Because

the stone's not lost. If my ex-maid's information is right, it's still at Camelot. Arthur must have taken it out before the battle as a precaution. He left it with Guinevere, and now your cousin has it."

"*Rhianna!*" Mordred clenched his fist in rage. He might have known King Arthur's daughter would stand in his way again. "We have to get it from her," he growled. "I need to raise another army."

"You don't need an army to catch a fly." His mother smiled. "Not even one that stings like your cousin. My ex-maid still has my mirror, so I can control her. This is what we'll do…"

◄ 1 ►

Witch Maid

A year long in Avalon Arthur slept
While his queen in fairest Camelot wept,
And a damsel with the Sword of Light
Fought shadows summoned by
the evil knight.

Rhianna fidgeted on the hard bench, fiddling with the ugly black pendant her mother had insisted she wear today in honour of her father's memory.

As princess of Camelot, she'd been given

a seat at the front, below the round window with its dragon design where Queen Guinevere had been kneeling for ages in a pool of red and gold autumn sunlight. The chapel was full, and in the hush she could hear people shifting their feet and coughing behind her.

She scowled at her mother's back, wishing she could go riding in the woods instead. It was exactly one year since her cousin Mordred had killed her father on the battlefield at Camlann and Merlin had brought the king's body through the mists to Avalon.

A *whole year* since she'd learned she was King Arthur's daughter, and she still hadn't completed her quest!

She swung her feet in their embroidered slippers in an effort to keep warm and wished she'd worn her boots instead. Her father wouldn't care if they looked silly with her dress.

The queen wore a simple blue gown with no jewellery. Copper hair, the same colour as Rhianna's, flowed loose around her shoulders. She was sobbing softly, which did strange things to Rhianna's insides. She felt embarrassed that her mother could cry before all these people. Then she felt guilty because she couldn't find any tears herself.

"My father's *not* dead," she muttered, touching his sword, Excalibur, which was lying on the bench beside her. "I've told you a hundred times! He's going to return to Camelot, just as soon as you let me out of here so I can look for the last two Lights and complete my quest…"

A touch on her shoulder made her jump. At first she thought it was her father's ghost, since he often appeared when she got upset. But it was just her friend Elphin, who had ridden through the mists with her from Avalon last year.

The Avalonian prince's eyes glowed violet as he leaned forward to whisper in her ear. "Let your mother pray for him if it makes her feel better," he said. "Then she'll be all the happier when we wake King Arthur and bring him back from Avalon, won't she?"

"*If* we ever manage to wake him! It's been a year, Elphin… a whole year!"

"A year in which you've won the Sword of Light from the Lady of the Lake, fought off a shadrake from Annwn, mended the Lance of Truth, rescued your mother from Mordred's dark tower, and been named heiress of Camelot." Elphin's lips twitched. "Father's right, you humans are much too impatient sometimes."

"That's because we haven't got as long to

live as you Avalonians," Rhianna said. But she smiled, too. Her friend was right. Though things at Camelot weren't as good as they might have been if Mordred hadn't killed her father, they were a lot better now than before she and Elphin had ridden through the mists.

"Don't worry," Elphin whispered, still teasing her. "I won't let Mordred kill you before you finish your quest."

"*I* won't let him kill me, you mean," Rhianna said. "I've got Excalibur, remember? But it'll be winter again soon, and the knights are hardly going to let us ride out on a quest to Dragonland in the middle of a snowstorm, are they? You saw how much snow there was last year. I think they're delaying so they'll have an excuse to stop me going."

Her voice had risen. "Shh!" Elphin said,

giving her shoulder a warning squeeze. "Your mother's looking at us."

The queen had finally stopped praying and turned to face the congregation. She frowned as she waited for Rhianna and Elphin to stop talking.

She cleared her throat and said, "Today we remember my lord Arthur Pendragon, who was slain by the traitor Prince Mordred on this day one year ago. Since the king cannot be with us in body, we'll honour his spirit, which still lives in his sword, Excalibur." She beckoned to Rhianna.

"Here we go," Rhianna muttered.

With a resigned sigh, she drew the Sword of Light from its red scabbard, which she wore at her left hip these days so she could draw the sword right-handed according to knightly code.

Feeling a bit self conscious, she went to stand beside her mother. She rested the point of the blade in the circle on the floor, where the squires would kneel to do their vigil before they became knights, and laid her hands on the white jewel set into Excalibur's hilt. The jewel warmed under her touch and began to shine faintly.

One by one, the knights walked up the aisle to kneel before Excalibur and renew their vows to their Pendragon. Sir Lancelot led them, his silver hair splashed with colour from the dragon window. He glanced up at the queen as he kissed the sword's hilt, and Rhianna saw her mother blush. "May King Arthur's spirit live forever!" he said loudly, before returning to his seat.

Sir Bors and Sir Agravaine were next, followed by the young knight, Sir Bedivere, whom everyone called 'Soft Hands'. Sir Bedivere winked at her and smiled in sympathy. "Soon be over, Damsel Rhianna," he whispered.

The ceremony went on and on. Rhianna's feet turned into little blocks of ice, and her arms ached with holding the blade still so that it wouldn't cut anyone. In battle, Excalibur's magic always made her feel stronger. But today, she could feel something working against the power of the sword.

She remembered feeling like this when she'd held its blade to Mordred's throat in the summer, and had a sudden sense of being watched. She peered suspiciously into the shadows at the back of the chapel and thought she saw a dark figure standing by the door.

"Come on, child," the priest said gently. "There are still a lot of people waiting."

Rhianna blinked and the figure vanished. She was being silly. Mordred would not dare come into Camelot's chapel alone, not after being captured and thrown into the dungeon the last time he was here.

Cai, the squire who had been with the knights sent to meet her when she rode through the mists from Avalon, was next in line. He had grown taller over the past few months, which made him seem less plump. Since she'd knighted him in the summer so he could be her champion and carry the Lance of Truth, Cai should really have come up first with Sir Lancelot, not last with the squires. But she was glad to see her friend's cheeky grin.

As the boy knelt, a draught flattened the candle flames and the air chilled. Before he could kiss Excalibur's jewel, the doors of the chapel suddenly blew open with a crash, making everyone jump.

Some of the damsels sitting at the back screamed. As people looked round to see who had interrupted the service, a girl with wild black hair covering her face came running up the aisle and launched herself at Rhianna.

Startled, Rhianna took a step back and lifted Excalibur. Then she recognised her maid Arianrhod and quickly lowered the sword, confused.

"Oi, witch's maid, watch it!" Before Arianrhod could attack Rhianna again, an older squire called Gareth grabbed the girl's hair and pushed her into the crowd. Arianrhod stumbled over a bench and fell to the floor beneath it, writhing and whimpering.

People crossed themselves. Cai tried to help

the girl. But everyone had crowded round to see what was wrong, and he couldn't get through.

The knights pushed through the crowd and picked the fallen bench off Arianrhod. "Get back!" Sir Bors bellowed. "Give the poor girl some air."

"Never mind air," a woman muttered. "It's fire that one wants. I always said you can't trust an ex-maid of Morgan Le Fay's. Keep her away from our princess, that's what I say!"

"Yeah," another agreed. "She just tried to kill Princess Rhianna."

"Nonsense," Sir Bedivere said, kneeling beside Arianrhod and catching her flailing wrists. "The noise scared her and she tripped, that's all. I think she's ill. Someone fetch Lady Isabel from the Damsel Tower."

"She was perfectly all right this morning," the first woman pointed out. "That wind wasn't natural, if you ask me – did you see that shadow flee out the door?"

People nodded and began to mutter about witchcraft.

Rhianna had heard enough.

She jumped on to the front bench. "Don't be so STUPID!" she shouted. Her voice, loud enough to be heard across a battlefield, echoed around the chapel. Excalibur's white jewel blazed in response.

Everyone stared at her, startled into silence.

"Arianrhod won't hurt me," Rhianna continued. "She's my friend! Let me through."

The queen frowned at her. "Get down from there, darling. This isn't the time or the place for battle stunts…"

Seeing that it would be the fastest way through the crowd, Rhianna had already kicked off her slippers and was leaping barefoot from bench to bench. She dropped beside Sir Bedivere, laid Excalibur down and knelt to comfort her friend.

Arianrhod clutched at Rhianna's dress, struggling to free herself from Sir Bedivere's grip.

The knight gave her a worried smile. "I daren't let go of her while she's like this, or she'll hurt herself," he said softly. "I think she might have hit her head when she tripped. We have to get her out of the chapel. There are too many people here."

"Maybe the priest can calm her down?" Sir Agravaine suggested.

Rhianna tried to catch Arianrhod's ankles,

but her friend's foot thumped into her cheek.

"Leave her to the knights, darling!" called the queen. "You'll get hurt."

Just as Rhianna wondered if she would get more bruises from her maid than she'd had from her enemies, otherworldly music tinkled around the chapel, making everyone smile. Elphin stood in the doorway, haloed by golden autumn sunshine. He had fetched his Avalonian harp, which he continued to play as he clambered over the benches to join them.

He looked down at Arianrhod. "*Sleep now*," he sang, magic in his voice. "*Sleep.*"

The girl's eyes closed, and she sank back to the floor. Sir Bedivere picked her up. The crowd sighed in relief.

Rhianna smoothed her dress and retrieved

Excalibur. "Take her up to my room," she ordered in a shaky voice.

Sir Bors shook his head. "I'm not sure that's the best idea, Damsel Rhianna."

"What's wrong? She's my maid. She's always in there, anyway. What's she going to do? Put a spell on me?"

The knights looked doubtfully at Arianrhod, who hung limply now in Sir Bedivere's arms, her dark hair trailing to the floor. The squires and damsels whispered uneasily. The priest looked uneasy, too. The queen didn't seem to know what to do.

"Oh, for goodness' sake!" Rhianna said. "Sir Bedivere can carry her up there. I give him permission. You're not going to attack any of the damsels, are you Sir Bedivere?"

The girls giggled as 'Soft Hands' blushed.

"No, Princess Rhianna," he said.

"Well then, that's settled. Put her in my bed. I'll be up to check on her as soon as we've finished my father's prayers."

This seemed to do the trick. People stopped muttering about witchcraft and remembered they were supposed to be praying for their king's soul.

The queen pulled herself together. "Rhianna's right. We can't let an attention-seeking maid disrupt my husband's service. Let's put this unfortunate interruption behind us. Who's next?"

The knights righted the benches, and everyone returned to their seats so the priest could bless them. Rhianna barely heard a word he said. She kept thinking of that dark figure she'd seen, before the doors had crashed open and Arianrhod attacked her.

Behind her, Elphin cradled his harp in his lap, a six-fingered hand resting across the strings to keep them quiet. He touched her shoulder. "Are you all right, Rhia?"

She nodded. "I think so." She raised a hand to feel her cheek where Arianrhod had kicked her, and realised that sometime during the struggle she'd lost her father's black pendant.

⁑

After the service, people gathered in the courtyard. Stalls had been set up serving roast boar and mead to those who couldn't fit inside the dining hall. Squires and servants hung about in groups in the autumn sunshine, discussing Arianrhod's strange behaviour and whether the maid could really be a witch like her first mistress. One of the older knights muttered about a trial by fire. The squires, overhearing this, began to gather sticks and bits of straw to build a bonfire so they could 'test' the other damsels, who screamed and fled towards the dining hall with the laughing boys in pursuit.

Rhianna elbowed through them all, chilled by their teasing. "Grow up!" she snapped at Gareth as she passed the squire. "How can you joke about burning someone? You know it's not Arianrhod's fault she had to serve Morgan Le Fay while the witch lived at Camelot."

She hadn't found her pendant in the short time she'd stayed behind in the chapel to look for it. One of the knights must have picked it up. She'd get it back later. Her friend was more important. She hurried to the Damsel Tower with Elphin at her heels.

Lady Isabel, the tall golden-haired woman who looked after the damsels, tried to stop the Avalonian boy at the door. But Rhianna seized his hand and pulled him inside. "I need him to play his harp to help Arianrhod get better," she explained breathlessly.

Lady Isabel shook her head. "First Sir Bedivere, and now a fairy prince! I don't know what Camelot is coming to since you arrived, Damsel Rhianna." She grabbed the back of Cai's tunic as the boy tried to follow them in. "Not you as well, young squire! I draw the line at two boys in Rhianna's room at once."

"But she needs my help, too," Cai protested. "I'm the Pendragon's champion. *And* I'm a knight now."

"All the more reason why I'm not letting you up there." Lady Isabel turned the boy around and marched him firmly back into the courtyard. "You go off to lunch, young knight. It's not like you to miss the chance of a good meal."

Cai pulled a face and looked up at the high windows of the tower in frustration. "Elphin's a lot more dangerous than me," he grumbled. "He might charm all the girls away to Avalon with his harp."

Rhianna smiled as she led the way up the stairs. "Just don't charm Arianrhod away until we find out what's wrong with her, will you?" she told her friend, pausing at the door to her chambers.

Elphin did not reply. He was looking past her, his eyes whirling purple. "That explains what happened to your father's pendant," he said in a wary tone.

They stared at the sleeping maid. Sir

Bedivere had put her on the bed and pulled a cover over her, but Arianrhod was trying to kick it off. She seemed to be having some kind of nightmare. Rhianna's missing pendant dangled from her hand, its chain wrapped about one slender wrist.

"It must have got tangled round her arm when I tried to help her in the chapel," she said in relief, rescuing the pendant. "She's having another bad dream, poor thing. Can you play your harp for her again?"

Ever since the guards had found the maid unconscious in the dungeon after Mordred's escape during the midsummer feast, Arianrhod had suffered from nightmares. No one knew exactly how she'd come to be down there. She claimed not to remember a thing.

Elphin ran his fingers over the strings, and

Arianrhod's back arched. She cried out in her sleep and mumbled something. They caught the words 'crown' and 'jewel' and 'Annwn'.

He lowered his harp and shook his head. "Sorry, Rhia. Something's working against my magic. I think she's under a spell."

"Morgan Le Fay again?" Mordred's mother had used the poor girl for a spell once before, cutting her cheek with a dagger and leaving a pentacle scar. Lady Morgan's spirit was in Annwn now, but the witch could still use her magic to reach the world of men.

"I don't know," Elphin said, still wary. "But your pendant's not black any more. Something's happening to the stone, look."

2

Arthur's Jewel

A single jewel Arthur left with his queen
When he rode to battle on Camlann's green.
Mordred's axe cut the fearless king down
The day a dragon stole Camelot's crown.

Rhianna hurried to the window and dangled the pendant against the sun. Although still dark, the stone no longer seemed ugly. A dim red light now flickered at its heart. Wondering if it had been damaged during the struggle in the chapel, she touched it and felt a slight heat.

"Careful, Rhia," Elphin warned. "We don't know where it came from yet."

Crown... jewel... Annwn... Arianrhod's words suddenly made sense.

"The Crown of Dreams, which hides the Jewel of Annwn!" She stared at Elphin, shivering with a mixture of excitement and terror. "That's what the song says, isn't it? The one Merlin sang for us in Avalon, when he brought my father's body through the mists? I should have realised before! My father gave this jewel to my mother the night before his last battle. She told me it turned black when he died, and you sensed an echo of magic in it the first time I showed it to you... Oh Elphin, I know it's only small but what if this is the *Jewel of Annwn*!"

She held the dark jewel at arm's length by its broken chain and looked at it with fresh eyes. Thank goodness she had kept it, and hadn't thrown it into Lady Nimue's lake as an offering as she had thought of doing at first.

But Elphin shook his head and said quietly, "If that were a thing of Annwn, I would not be able to touch it without pain, Rhia."

"But you didn't touch it, did you?"

"I touched it when you wore it at the Midsummer Feast, remember?"

"I'd forgotten that. But it was still black then, so maybe its magic wasn't working properly. We have to show it to Merlin!"

They went through to Rhianna's sitting room, where a small, grey-blue falcon was leashed to a perch under the window. No one had cleaned in here this morning, and feathers spiralled up from the floor. Rhianna pulled off the bird's hood and rested her hand on Excalibur's hilt so she could talk to Merlin. The druid's spirit had been trapped inside the little merlin falcon since Morgan Le Fay drowned his man's body on their way over from Avalon last year.

The bird fluffed its feathers, making Rhianna sneeze. "Have you brought my breakfast?" he grumbled. "No one's fed me this morning. Where is everyone?"

"The damsels will be back soon, Merlin," Elphin said with a smile. "I expect they'll bring you some meat from the feast." He ran a slender finger down the speckled breast. The merlin shivered in pleasure and nibbled at his knuckle.

Rhianna sighed. "When you two have quite finished grooming each other, we've got something to show you, Merlin."

She opened her hand to reveal the pendant. Merlin gave it a keen stare. She felt sure he recognised the stone. But as she tried to decide if it had changed colour again, the bird turned its back on her and returned to his grooming. "Put that thing away, Rhianna Pendragon," he grumbled. "I'm not interested in your baubles. Go and show it to the damsels, foolish girl."

She checked the door to make sure they were alone, and lowered her voice. "You might be interested in this one. We think this is the Jewel of Annwn."

"Whatever gave you that idea?" The merlin stretched a wing and eyed Elphin in amusement. "The Jewel of Annwn, she says…

as if such a thing could be worn around her neck without stealing the breath from her throat, or lie against a mortal heart without stopping it stone dead. Even set into the Crown, Annwn's jewel is dangerous enough, but there at least, the rightful heir to the throne can wear it without fear of dying."

Rhianna felt faintly disappointed. She frowned at the stone and scrunched up the chain to put it back into her pocket. "Then it's just some old pendant my mother gave me, after all. I thought when it changed colour like it did—"

"It *what*?" Merlin turned round so quickly he almost fell off his perch. "Let me see."

"You wanted me to put it away just now," Rhianna said, irritated. "Make up your mind."

"Hold Excalibur closer," the druid instructed.

"That's better. Now then, let's have a proper look." He twisted his head to examine the stone with each eye in turn. "Hmm, mmm... ah yes, I see now. This isn't Annwn's jewel, you silly girl – it's Arthur's. Seems your father's secrets did not die with him, after all."

"What secrets?" she asked.

The bird fluffed its feathers again, grumpily. "If I knew that, they wouldn't be secrets, would they? Only another Pendragon can look into the king's jewel and see the secrets he stored inside."

Rhianna frowned. "So why can't I see them? I've got Pendragon blood."

"Because, Rhianna Pendragon, its magic won't work by itself. You'll have to put it back into your father's crown before you understand."

"So Rhianna's right – this stone *did* come

from the Crown of Dreams," Elphin said. "I sensed its power before, but never thought it might have come from one of the four Lights! Why didn't the queen tell us what it was? Didn't she know?"

"Of course not," the merlin said. "If she'd known what it really was, she'd have been too scared to accept it. I told Arthur to take it out of the Crown before the battle in case things went badly – and a good thing I did! As far as Guinevere was concerned, it was a parting gift from her loving husband. I counted on its ugliness to keep it safe from any light-fingered maids. While Arthur's jewel is here with us, no impostor can use its magic to take the throne. But that light you can see inside means the Crown has been found… Hmm. This changes things."

Rhianna had been thinking of Arianrhod's fingers on the pendant. But when Merlin said the Crown had been found, she instantly forgot her friend's strange behaviour. "Who's found it?" she said. "If it's Mordred, we've failed! I need all four Lights to bring my father back from Avalon…"

"You're not listening, as usual." Merlin pecked at her hand again, almost making her drop the pendant. "I never said you needed all four Lights to bring Arthur back to the world of men – but it's true he'll need as many of them as possible if he's to defeat the dark knight and restore Camelot to its former glory when he does return. I'd hoped the Sword and the Lance might be enough to lure his soul back into his body. Arthur never possessed the Grail anyway, and while the Crown was buried in a dragon's lair, it was safe enough from enemy hands until he came back to reclaim it. But now the Crown has been found, which changes things. Without your father's jewel in place, it won't work properly and it's dangerous to wear. But it's the Pendragon crown and it contains the secrets of the old Dragonlords, so Mordred might be able to use it against us if he gets hold of it. You need to go to Dragonland and get it back as soon as possible."

"That's what I've been telling my mother and the knights for months!" Rhianna said in frustration. "But they won't listen to me. They keep saying they can't leave Camelot unprotected to ride out on another quest, in case Mordred's planning to attack the castle with a new army. They don't seem to understand I need to find the Crown before he does.

Will you fly in to the Round Table meeting again, Merlin, and talk to them all again like you did in the spring? If you tell them what you just told us, they'll have to let me go and look for it!"

"Let *us* go," Elphin corrected. "You're not going anywhere without me and Cai."

Rhianna grinned. "All right, us." She pulled a face at the little hawk. "I suppose we'll have to take Merlin as well to show us the way..."

Shouts in the courtyard below the window distracted them. Merlin fluttered up and down his perch. "What's going on out there?" he grumbled. "Rather a lot of noise for a memorial service, if you ask me."

"They've been drinking mead," Elphin said, his eyes purple with disapproval. "It's probably another fight."

Then they heard feet pounding up the stairs and Lady Isabel's angry shout. Rhianna drew Excalibur as Gareth, the squire who had called Arianrhod a witch in the chapel, burst into the room.

"Damsel Rhianna, you got to come quick!" he puffed. "There's a man in black armour outside who says he's come for Arianrhod, and Cai's challenged him to a duel!"

A chill went down Rhianna's back as she remembered the shadowy figure she'd seen in the chapel before Arianrhod had attacked her.

"Mordred!" she breathed, staring at Elphin.

Her friend shook his head. "He wouldn't dare come alone, not after what happened at midsummer. And anyway, Cai's got more sense than to challenge Prince Mordred to a duel."

"I'm not so sure." She thought of how proud

Cai had been when she knighted him last year.

"Young Sir Cai, the shortest knight who ever lived, duelling?" The merlin let out a screech that sounded suspiciously like a bird-laugh. "That'll be something to see! Take me outside."

"It's not *funny*!" Rhianna said, rushing to the window. "Cai's going to get himself killed out there."

"Cai's going to get hurt," Gareth agreed. "That's a real war lance the challenger's carrying, not a wooden jousting spear."

Rhianna leaned out to see the jousting field where, in the spring, the squires had tilted for fun. Today, the autumn sun cast long shadows across the course from the wall, and at first she couldn't see anyone. Then she saw Cai's pony, Sandy, gallop out of the gates with his mane glowing like fire.

The boy still wore his squire's uniform, but he carried the Lance of Truth, which left a trail of glitter through the air. After him ran a crowd of eager squires, cheering him on, followed by the adults from the courtyard shouting at them to stop. At the far end of the field, a shaggy black horse reared as the stranger raised his lance to answer Cai's challenge.

Rhianna tried to see if the man had a crippled leg and one hand like her cousin, but he was too far away.

Gareth jostled behind her, trying to see as well. "I'd say the maid's as good as his," he said.

"Oh stop it, Gareth!" Rhianna said, wondering why he'd run all the way up the Damsel Tower to warn them if he disliked her friends so much. She sheathed Excalibur and scowled at the boy. "If you want to make yourself useful, go and saddle Alba for me. I've got to get changed, and I'm not doing it with you in here."

Gareth looked alarmed. "Saddle your fairy horse? Not me!"

"I'll do it, Rhia," Elphin said, slinging his harp over one shoulder and pulling Gareth out of the room. "Better be quick changing, though. They're not hanging about out there."

Rhianna saw the knights' big horses gallop out of the gates and set out across the field after Cai's pony. She relaxed slightly as she recognised Sir Bedivere's chestnut, Sir Agravaine's black, and Sir Lancelot's white stallion.

"A knight who carries the Lance of Truth cannot be killed," Merlin said. "Where are you going, Rhianna Pendragon? Let the lad take care of it—"

His words ended in another screech as she fixed the hood back over the druid's head.

Rhianna hurried back to her bedroom and found Arianrhod at the window, woken by the noise. Her friend swung round with frightened eyes. "Who's that man out there?" she asked. "Why is Gareth saying he wants me? I had a horrible dream about my old mistress Lady Morgan… she didn't send him, did she?"

"Don't worry, we won't let him touch you, whoever he is," she told the maid, opening her clothing chest and pulling out her armour. "And Lady Morgan's dead now, you know that. Stay here."

Lady Isabel had reached the top of the stairs. She pressed a hand to her side and frowned at Rhianna and Arianrhod. "I don't know what's been going on up here…" she began.

Then she noticed what was happening outside the window. "Is that young Sir Cai on his pony? What does he think he's doing? The queen specifically said no jousting today."

"Don't worry, Lady Isabel, Cai's not going to joust," Rhianna said, already out of her dress. She pulled on her riding leggings and slipped her Avalonian armour over the top. The silvery material fell to just above her knees, light enough to dance in, yet strong enough to stop an arrow. Finally, she buckled Excalibur around her waist. Feeling much more comfortable than she had done in the chapel, she hurried down the stairs after the boys.

"Damsel Rhianna!" Lady Isabel said, losing patience. "Where do you think you're going dressed like that? Your mother's expecting you at lunch."

"I'll have lunch later!" Rhianna called back over her shoulder. "I've got a duel to stop."

3

The Challenge

A stranger came on Arthur's Day
To claim the maid of Morgan Le Fay.
So Camelot's champion rode out to fight
One boy and his lance against a knight.

On her way down the stairs, Rhianna wondered what she'd do if the challenger under that battered helm did turn out to be her cousin Mordred. But Elphin was right. Mordred wouldn't come to Camelot alone, not after the last time, when he'd been captured and thrown in the dungeon.

She clenched her fist on Excalibur's hilt. Whoever it was out there, she wouldn't let him hurt Arianrhod or Cai.

Her beloved mist horse, Alba, waited for her in the courtyard, saddled and bridled. Elphin was already mounted on Evenstar. The two Avalonian horses shone in the shadows, their white manes rippling almost to their knees, and their silver-shod hooves pawing the castle yard.

Are we going home now? Alba said, whinnying when she saw Rhianna.

"Soon, my beautiful one." She gave the mare's nose a quick stroke before springing into the saddle. She felt bad every time Alba asked that, because she knew the little horse meant home to Avalon. It had been a whole year since either of them had tasted apples from Lord Avallach's orchard. "We're going racing instead," she said. "You'll enjoy that, won't you?"

Alba shook her mane in excitement. *I will win today. I am very fast.*

Rhianna smiled.

"Rhia," Elphin said, nodding at the gates, which had begun to close. "We'd better hurry if we're going to get out."

Men came running out of the dining hall to man the walls. She saw bows and arrows in their hands as well as half-eaten pies, and her stomach clenched. What if Mordred had come with his army, after all? She drew Excalibur and trotted Alba towards the gates. Elphin followed with his harp on his back.

"Sorry, Princess Rhianna," one of the guards said, stepping into her path and raising his spear. "We've orders to keep you inside until we find out who that stranger is."

"Out of my way, you fool!" Rhianna said impatiently. "Cai's out there. You can't let him tilt against a grown man. He'll be killed!"

"The boy carries the magic lance, and that stranger doesn't look like much of a knight," the guard said with a glance at his friend. "We think young Sir Cai'll be all right."

"Then you're idiots!" Rhianna gathered up her reins and headed Alba towards the shrinking gap between the gates. She closed her eyes as they loomed closer.

"Mist, Alba," she whispered. "Mist."

The guards yelled in alarm when they realised she was not going to stop, and jumped out of her way. She heard Elphin's harp tinkle across the courtyard, and something solid brushed her shoulder. Her skin prickled. She opened her eyes to see Excalibur's jewel shining brightly. Then Alba was through the gates and galloping down the slope towards the jousting field, with Evenstar close on her heels. She glanced back over her shoulder and saw Gareth squeeze through the gap and run after them. The gates shut behind the squire with a dull boom.

"You're crazy, Rhia!" Elphin called. "You can't mist through the closed gates of Camelot! If they'd shut them all the way, you and Alba would both have broken necks by now, and I'd be taking your body back to the crystal caverns to lie with your father's."

She grimaced. "They didn't shut them, did they? They knew they'd be in more trouble with my mother if they hurt me than if they let me out. Is that man one of Mordred's bloodbeards, do you think?"

The challenger didn't look crippled like her cousin, but Mordred might have used magic to make himself appear whole. His helm was closed so nobody could see his face.

Elphin frowned. "I can't tell from here. Surely the knights aren't going to let Cai go through with this?"

Despite the closed gates, a surprising number of people had managed to get out of Camelot to watch. They climbed on to the stands beside the jousting field, where, normally, pavilions would be set up and seats draped with flags and banners. Today, there were no colourful flags and no cheers. The crowd watched in silence as Cai trotted his pony to one end of the field, and the challenger trotted his horse to the other.

The boy looked scared, but gripped his lance in a determined fashion. The stranger laughed.

At first Rhianna wondered if the knights planned to teach Cai a lesson, as they had done with her at the spring joust when she'd tilted against Sir Bedivere. Were they counting on the boy to pull out and let a grown knight take his place? Then she saw Sir Bors and Sir Agravaine quietly trotting their horses up behind the stands, out of view of the stranger. Sir Lancelot waited at the other side of the course with more knights.

"Clever. They're going to trap him when he's made his run before he can recover his balance," Elphin said. "Cai's just got to duck. He'll be all right, Rhia, don't worry – I'll help him, like I did before." He balanced his harp on Evenstar's withers and readied his fingers over the strings.

Sir Bedivere mounted the stand with a trumpet. He announced, "The stranger claims Princess Rhianna's maid Arianrhod belongs to him. The Pendragon's champion says the stranger's wrong. This tilt will decide the matter, according to Camelot's law." He checked the positions of the knights creeping up behind the stands and noticed the two mist horses standing in the shadows. He shook his head urgently at Rhianna as he lifted the trumpet to his lips.

"He means don't interfere," Elphin whispered.

Rhianna gripped Excalibur tighter. "I know, but I'm not going to let that man kill Cai!" she hissed.

A blast rang out, and the black horse sprang into a gallop. Sandy was only a few heartbeats behind. The stranger lowered his lance. After a bit of a fumble, Cai managed to lower the Lance of Truth, which sparkled brighter as Elphin played his harp. Sir Bors and Sir Agravaine fixed their eyes on the challenger and drew their swords as he galloped closer.

"Duck, Cai!" Sir Bedivere called.

But Cai didn't seem to hear. He gripped the Lance of Truth as if it were his only friend in the world. He was getting too big for his pony, Rhianna noticed – and too big to duck a lowered lance easily.

"Race Sandy for me, Alba!" she shouted, urging the mare down the course after Cai's pony. The crowd gasped as she galloped out into the sun with Excalibur shining in her right hand. Sir Bedivere shouted something she didn't hear above the pounding hooves.

"Cai!" she yelled. "Pull up, you idiot!"

Sunlight flashed into her eyes, half blinding her. Cai didn't hear her any more than he'd heard Sir Bedivere. Squinting from behind him, she could see he had the Lance of Truth aimed straight at his opponent's shield. She had to admire her friend's bravery. But if he didn't pull up, he would die.

Elphin's harp sang out louder across the field. Excalibur warmed in her hand. Its jewel glowed brighter and its blade left a trail of light through the air. The Lance of Truth brightened, too, maybe sensing the Sword nearby. In front of them, the black horse loomed larger against the setting sun with every stride.

"Faster, Alba!" she yelled.

I will win this race, the mare snorted.

The mist horse's nose caught up with Sandy's tail, then Cai's knee. Finally, the boy noticed Alba. He gave Rhianna a startled look.

"Damsel Rhianna!" he gasped, as she leaned across and grabbed his rein to pull the pony out of the other horse's path. "Don't—"

Too late.

There was a blinding flash as the Lance of Truth clashed with the challenger's lance. Somehow Excalibur got caught between them, and went spinning out of her grip. The crowd gasped in horror as Alba misted under her to avoid the weapons. Sandy, being a sensible sort of pony, shied out of the way too, unseating Cai, whose saddle slipped sideways. Then the challenger was past them. Splinters of his lance showered around them as the ground rushed up to meet Rhianna.

Cai fell on top of her with a grunt and they rolled together in the mud. Rhianna closed her eyes, feeling sick. They ended up in a tangle of limbs against the central barrier and lay still, catching their breath.

"Are you hurt, Damsel Rhianna?" Cai asked in a shaky voice.

"I'm still alive, no thanks to you," she muttered, sitting up and rubbing her shoulder.

She looked anxiously for Excalibur. The sword stuck out of the mud nearby, thankfully undamaged. She got shakily to her feet, wiped the blade clean on her leg and sheathed it. Sandy and Alba came trotting back together. Both horses looked sheepish.

I am sorry I misted, Alba said. *I thought you held the shining sword, so you would stay on me.*

"I did, until my so-called champion here knocked it out of my hand with the Lance of Truth," Rhianna said.

Cai flushed, rubbing his wrist. "I wouldn't have done, if you hadn't put Excalibur in the way," he said. "I'd have knocked that dirty spy off his horse instead! He wasn't even a proper knight. Why did you stop me?"

"He'd have skewered you first, more like. You are an idiot Cai! Why didn't you let Sir Lancelot challenge him?"

"I'm supposed to be your champion now! Any rate, Sir Lancelot's still angry with Arianrhod for letting Mordred out of the dungeon in the summer, so he wouldn't have jousted to save her from that man."

"He wouldn't have let an untrained squire joust in his place."

"I'm not untrained!" Cai's flush deepened. "I've been practising every day since you knighted me. If you hadn't stopped me just then, the Lance's magic would have worked, I'm sure of it."

At the other end of the barrier, the stranger had been surrounded by angry knights. Sir Agravaine and Sir Bors dragged him off his horse and quickly disarmed him. They pulled off his helm, none too gently. Everyone went quiet as they looked at the challenger's face.

Rhianna clenched her fist on Excalibur. To her relief, it wasn't her cousin. But she'd recognise that horrible scar anywhere. It was Mordred's bloodbeard captain, who had almost killed her twice now, and tortured Sir Bors last winter in the Saxon camp. A dragon had clawed his face during the battle that followed, but he hadn't died. His mouth twisted into a sneer when he saw Rhianna staring, and he spat into the mud.

"Is that who I think it is, Rhia?" Elphin asked, trotting Evenstar across to join them.

She nodded, chilled.

Sir Bors obviously recognised him too, because he clouted the bloodbeard on the ear, knocking him into the mud. "That's for what you did to me last year," the big knight growled, putting his boot on the captive's neck. "Where's Prince Mordred and your blood-drinking friends?"

The bloodbeard bared his teeth. "W-wouldn't you like to know?"

"What do you want with Princess Rhianna's maid?"

"She served my master's mother, Lady

Morgan Le Fay. Mordred wants a word with her. You all saw me unseat the Pendragon's champion – according to Camelot's law, I believe that means you must hand the maid over to me."

The crowd began to mutter.

"Bloody cheek, him coming here invoking King Arthur's laws!"

"The maid *did* let the dark knight escape at midsummer, though."

"We don't want Mordred's lot coming down here again. Maybe it'd be easiest to let him take the girl?"

"Nobody's taking Arianrhod anywhere," Rhianna said firmly, leading Alba across to the knights and their prisoner. "Least of all that man!"

She appealed to Sir Bors. "Can't you see,

Mordred sent his bloodbeard here to stir up trouble? You can't possibly believe him! Elphin thinks Arianrhod's under a spell."

"Ha, so you'd believe a *fairy* now? Since when have Lord Avallach's people cared about men's affairs?" The bloodbeard sneered at the Avalonian boy, who watched silently from a distance, clutching his harp.

Sir Bedivere took her by the elbow. "Don't get too close, Damsel Rhianna," he warned. "He seems to have come alone, but it might be a trick."

"It's a trick, all right! Arianrhod's innocent."

"Seems the witch-maid's put a spell on your princess, too," said the bloodbeard in a sly tone. "What's happened to King Arthur's famous laws? Does every man who comes to Camelot in good faith get challenged to a duel, and then

– when he wins in a fair tilt – get dragged off his horse and arrested by Camelot's knights?"

The crowd muttered again.

"He does, when he's the same man who commanded the traitor's army," Sir Bors grunted. He wrenched their captive's arms behind his back and hauled him to his feet. "Come on, scum. Maybe we'll get some answers out of you after you've spent a night in the dungeon."

"This proves King Arthur's dreams for Camelot are dead!" the bloodbeard shouted as he was marched away. The crowd watched him go, still muttering uneasily.

Sir Bedivere sighed. He gave Rhianna's shoulder a squeeze as they followed the knights. "We'll get to the bottom of this, Damsel Rhianna, don't worry. That was a brave thing you did out there. I thought young Cai was going to get himself skewered, as well. Don't know what's got into the boy lately – he seems to think a magic lance can turn a squire into a champion knight without all the hard work in-between. In fact, he's rather like a damsel I know, who thinks a magic sword can turn a girl into a Pendragon…"

He eyed Excalibur's muddy blade in amusement and lowered his voice. "Next time, use your left hand if you're in trouble. Staying alive is more important than knightly codes."

Rhianna flushed. "I've fought more battles than Cai has."

Sir Bedivere stared after their prisoner and sighed. "I know you have, Damsel Rhianna. And I've a feeling there will be a few more to fight before Camelot's safe from the dark knight. Prince Mordred obviously hasn't given up yet."

4

Round Table Meeting

In Dragonland the crown lies hidden
Where Mordred and his men have ridden,
And druids of old breathed their last
Keeping the secrets of Pendragons past.

After the excitement of the challenge and the capture of Mordred's captain, Camelot was in uproar. Some people said that the duel was a disgrace on Arthur's Day, while others blamed Arianrhod for bringing the bloodbeard into their midst in the first place. The knights were jumpy about security and doubled the guard on the gates.

As they rode back into the castle, Rhianna tried to tell Sir Bedivere what Merlin had said about her father's crown. But the knight they called 'Soft Hands' wouldn't listen to her. "We've more important things to think about now, Damsel Rhianna," he told her. "Your poor mother's upset enough, what with that bloodbeard ruining Arthur's Day and you flinging yourself on the end of his lance like you did, without worrying her about jewels and crowns."

"But it's not just any crown!" Rhianna said. "Don't you understand? It's the Crown of Dreams, the third *Light*!"

"And if you want to keep the first two Lights, you'll let us deal with this new threat from Mordred before we do anything else," Sir Bedivere said with uncharacteristic firmness. "Go see to your horse, and leave the fighting to us men, for once." He shook his head at her and went off to supervise the squires, who were excitedly discussing the duel instead of getting on with their work.

As a last resort, she tried to find her mother to tell her that the jewel in her pendant had come out of King Arthur's crown. But the queen had retired to her rooms with Sir Lancelot and would not answer the door.

"She's not very pleased with you for missing King Arthur's special lunch," Lady Isabel said, giving Rhianna's muddy armour a disapproving look. "Probably best to let her calm down a bit before you see her."

Rhianna retreated to her room in frustration, where she found Arianrhod sobbing on the bed. She spent the rest of that afternoon reassuring her friend that the bloodbeard had been taken to the dungeons and couldn't hurt her, then giving Merlin a blow by blow account of the duel, by which time it was too late to do anything except fall asleep with her hair still full of mud from the jousting field.

※

Rhianna woke with a stiff neck to find the Damsel Tower buzzing with fresh gossip. It turned out the knights had spent the night questioning their prisoner, and Queen Guinevere had called a meeting of the

Round Table straight after breakfast.

"I haven't time to eat all that now," she said, pushing away the laden tray Arianrhod had brought her and leaping out of bed. "I mustn't be late for the meeting!"

Arianrhod immediately started fussing about the state of Rhianna's dress, which had been flung into a corner yesterday when Rhianna had changed into her armour to help Cai.

"Leave it!" Rhianna snapped as Arianrhod tried to drag a brush through her tangled hair. "It doesn't matter what I look like. I want to hear what they found out from that bloodbeard, and why he wanted you."

A herald in the courtyard below her window announced the meeting was about to start.

"I've got to go," she said, snatching an apple from the tray. "You stay up here, all right? Then you'll be safe. Lady Isabel won't let any strange men into the Damsel Tower – you know what she's like."

Arianrhod managed a little smile. "I'm sorry, Rhia," she sniffed.

"What for?"

"For attacking you in the chapel."

"That wasn't your fault." Rhianna buckled her sword belt over her dress, distracted by the knights hurrying across the yard towards the Great Hall. "Elphin says you were under a spell. We'll talk about this later, when the meeting's finished. You can get a bath ready for me."

Arianrhod brightened up immediately. "Shall I bring up lunch from the kitchens, too?" she said. "So we can eat while we talk?"

"Whatever you like." Impatient with the

domestic details, Rhianna hurried down the spiral stair, munching the apple.

She paused before the big doors of the Great Hall to get rid of the apple core, smooth her skirt and run her fingers through her hair. A pile of swords waited outside the door. The knights were already inside, taking their seats around the circular slab of blue stone marked with druid-spirals, but the queen had not arrived yet. She straightened Excalibur – the only sword allowed into a Round Table meeting – and took a deep breath before she entered.

Sir Bors, Sir Agravaine and Sir Lancelot stood at one side of the hall in the shadows, arguing. She caught the words *Dragonland* and *Mordred*. Then Sir Lancelot said, "Shh!" and turned his strange pale gaze upon her. Seeing her, the other two lowered their voices.

Rhianna marched past them with her head held high. She took her usual place at the Round Table, next to her mother's seat.

Sir Bedivere picked a grass seed out of her hair as he took the seat on her other side. "The queen's still at breakfast," he said quietly. "You've time to snatch a few bites, if you're hungry."

"I've already had breakfast," Rhianna said, thinking of the apple. "What are Sir Lancelot and the others talking about? Is it to do with that bloodbeard? Arianrhod said you questioned him last night. Did he talk?"

Sir Bedivere grimaced at the three older knights. "I wasn't involved, but I expect we'll find out soon enough. Ah, here she is."

Queen Guinevere swept through the doors, wearing a green silk gown trimmed with gold. A tiara twinkled in her hair as she walked through a sunbeam that was slanting through the hole in the roof above the Round Table. She'd regained her beauty since her imprisonment in Mordred's dark tower, and all the men's eyes followed her.

Rhianna wished her mother would move faster so they could start. But just before the big doors swung shut, a plump figure squeezed through with a half-eaten honey-cake in his hand, distracting everyone.

"Cai!" she said with a flush of pleasure. This was the first meeting of the Round Table since she'd knighted her friend up at the lake. She'd forgotten he could join them now.

The knights blinked at the boy as he hesitated near the doors. It seemed they had forgotten, too.

"Well, come in then, young Sir Cai," Sir

Bedivere said, smiling. "Take a seat. We've got a few vacancies, thanks to Mordred's lot up at the North Wall."

"The boy's too young!" protested Sir Agravaine. "We've got important matters to discuss this morning."

The queen had been frowning at the state of Rhianna's hair. She turned her frown on Cai as he began to slide into one of the big chairs. "What's that squire doing in here?" she asked in a confused tone.

"Cai's a knight now, Mother," Rhianna reminded her.

Sir Bors cleared his throat and said, "Cai, I know that you've been knighted, but the next meeting might be more suitable for your first time with us. Agravaine's right. We'll be discussing the things we've learned from that bloodbeard we caught yesterday, and they're not pretty."

"If I'm old enough to hear it, then Cai's old enough," Rhianna said firmly. "Without him and the Lance of Truth, you wouldn't have caught that bloodbeard in the first place. He'd still be creeping about Camelot, spying on us all."

"I know what you're going to talk about, any rate," Cai said, glancing at her. "You tortured the prisoner last night, didn't you? All the squires are saying so. We heard his screams."

Some of the knights frowned.

"Now, you know very well King Arthur forbade the use of torture at Camelot, Cai," Sir Lancelot said. "Just squires' gossip," he reassured the queen. "You know what they're like."

Guinevere frowned too. But then she sighed and said, "I suppose what we've got to discuss today is no worse than squires' gossip. He can stay, if he promises not to tell all his friends what goes on in here. You understand, young Cai? What is spoken of at the Round Table is for the ears of Camelot's knights and those of Pendragon blood only."

Cai nodded solemnly.

Sir Bors gave him a doubtful look. "Right," he said. "We've wasted enough time. Sit over there and keep quiet, Cai. If you open your mouth just once, I'll throw you out myself, get it?"

Cai nodded again. He grinned at Rhianna and quickly stuffed the rest of his breakfast into his mouth before anyone could tell him off for eating at the Round Table.

Rhianna had hoped to learn what the bloodbeard wanted with Arianrhod, but the knights seemed more interested in the information he'd given them about Mordred. Sir Lancelot stood up and gave an account of the interrogation, interrupted now and again by Sir Agravaine.

When they'd finished, the men muttered uneasily.

"So it seems Mordred's holed up in Dragonland," Sir Lancelot said. "I wondered where he'd got to after he escaped from our dungeon at midsummer. He's probably avoiding the roads and working his way back north. I propose we go after him and cut him off before he reaches the North Wall. If we can trap him in Dragonland without his army, we should be able to finish off the traitor once and for all."

The older knights nodded in agreement.

"I agree. Let's put an end to all this stupid wrangling over the throne," Sir Agravaine said. "We don't need Mordred now we've got Rhianna. I say we kill the dark knight and have done with it."

Queen Guinevere frowned. "And leave Camelot unprotected?"

"Mordred's hiding like a frightened rabbit in Dragonland," Lancelot continued. "We routed his army in the north, and we're at peace with the Saxons now, thanks to our princess here, so there should be no threat to Camelot while we're gone. If you need us, my lady, light the druid beacons and we'll return at once. We shouldn't be long. The prisoner will soon tell us where his master's hiding now we've loosened his tongue."

But Sir Bedivere said, "I don't like it. What if the bloodbeard's lying? That nonsense about Damsel Rhianna's maid could be just a smokescreen. What if he came here to lead us into a trap? And what about the dragons?"

This set off more grumbling. A grizzled old knight said, "The maid's probably part of it. We should question her, too."

"No!" Rhianna said, her stomach doing strange things. If Mordred was in Dragonland, then that would be the perfect excuse for the third part of her quest. All she had to do was make sure the knights didn't leave her behind. "Arianrhod's got nothing to do with this. I think I know what Mordred wants..."

"We never found out who her parents were, did we?" continued the old knight. "Mighty convenient, how we found her abandoned on that hillside as a baby. The witch planned for the long term, we know that now. What if she planted the girl in Camelot as a spy to be brought up here among us hearing all our secrets, and now his mother's dead, Mordred wants the maid back so she can tell him everything she's learned about us?"

"Don't be silly!" Rhianna said, but she couldn't help thinking of her friend being found senseless in the dungeon after Mordred escaped. And Arianrhod herself had told her how she'd been found as a baby, abandoned outside Camelot's gates. She couldn't believe her friend would betray them, though.

"The maid's not important," Sir Lancelot said firmly. "Mordred's man didn't even get to see her, so let's not get distracted. If we take all our knights, we should be able to deal with the traitor, even if it is a trap. We know Mordred hasn't had time to raise another army. At most he'll have a few bloodbeards with him, and if there's enough of us we'll be able to handle them and any dragons that might show up. I doubt there's many of the creatures left these days, anyway."

"There's at least one," Rhianna said, thinking of the shadrake that had attacked them last year. "And I think I know why Mordred's gone there – my father's crown is in Dragonland too."

The knights stared at her.

"The Crown of Dreams is in Dragonland?" Sir Lancelot said. "How do you know?"

"A little bird told me." Rhianna smiled sweetly at them, enjoying herself now she had their attention.

Cai grinned, seeing the joke.

"She means Merlin," Sir Bedivere explained for the benefit of those who did not know how the druid had escaped Morgan Le Fay's ambush. "His spirit lives in the body of a hawk now."

"So *that's* why Mordred went to Dragonland!" Sir Bors said. "The little devil's cleverer than we thought. A dragon stole the crown from the battlefield after Arthur died – where else would it have taken its treasure? It's probably got a lair somewhere in the hills."

"Yes," Rhianna said. She fumbled in her pocket for the black pendant and started to explain about King Arthur's jewel, but the men weren't interested in the dull-looking stone.

"The prisoner didn't say nothing about a crown," Sir Agravaine said, scowling.

"Good," Sir Bors grunted. "Then at least we know Mordred hasn't found it yet."

"That bloodbeard's lying through his rotten teeth, more like," growled Agravaine. "He talked too quickly for my liking. I said we should have used more persuasive methods to loosen his tongue."

The knights began to argue about the best way of doing this. Cai listened eagerly, but Rhianna felt a bit sick.

She was glad when the queen leaned across and touched the pendant. "This jewel came from Arthur's crown?" her mother whispered. "I never knew… why didn't he tell me? I just thought it was a magic stone that changed colour when he died."

"Maybe he wanted you to keep his secrets safe?" she said, too embarrassed to tell

Guinevere the real reason her father had been sparing with the truth. "I have to go with them, Mother! I have to get the Crown of Dreams back. It's one of the four Lights my father will need to defeat Mordred when he returns to Camelot."

"Oh no, darling." The queen shook her head. "This is a war party. There might be fighting."

"I can fight! I've been training to use Excalibur in my right hand like a proper knight." Rhianna stood on her chair so she could draw her sword to demonstrate. The blade glimmered faintly as it sensed the magic of the Round Table. This got the knights' full attention, and she announced, "I'm coming with you! I've got Pendragon blood – I can speak to the dragons if you need me to."

She expected another argument. But Sir Bors merely sighed and said, "Sit down, Damsel Rhianna. Don't worry, we're not leaving you behind – you and your friends will only ride after us like you did last time, and then Mordred will just pick you off one by one. I'm taking you with me, where I can keep an eye on you. If we see a dragon, we might need Excalibur's magic. But you'll stay out of the fighting this time, even if I have to tie you to a tree to keep you out of it."

Rhianna grinned.

"Does that mean I can come, too?" Cai asked, his eyes shining. "I'm the Pendragon's champion now, and I've got the magic lance."

"Cai, shut it," Sir Agravaine warned. "Of course you're coming. We'll need someone to groom our horses."

The queen shook her head again. "Take the squire and the Lance of Truth with you if you must, but you're *not* taking my daughter into those wilds everyone knows are crawling with druids and dragons – and now, it seems, Mordred's bloodbeards as well! I forbid it."

"You can't keep me here, Mother," Rhianna said, her blood rising. "Sir Bors is right. I'll just ask Elphin to help me with his magic again, and we'll ride across the Summer Sea after them. Besides, you said I could go and look for my father's crown, didn't you?"

"That was when Mordred was safely locked up in Camelot's dungeon, not loose in Dragonland with God knows what riff-raff he's persuaded to help him this time," the queen said. "Be sensible, Rhianna darling. The knights can easily look for Arthur's crown on their way to get Mordred. After all, they know what it looks like, and you don't."

Before Rhianna could explain about the song pictures in Avalon, and how Merlin had shown them the first three Lights in the crystal walls of Lord Avallach's palace, Sir Lancelot put a hand on Guinevere's arm and whispered something into her ear. The queen gave Rhianna an exasperated look.

The silver-haired knight slammed his hand down on the table for attention.

"We've discussed this long enough," Sir Lancelot said. "If Princess Rhianna's right about Arthur's crown being in Dragonland too, then we can't delay. We have to go after Mordred before he finds it, because if he discovers how to use its magic to control dragons like the old Pendragons used to do, then having an army won't help us very much. I thought we'd have more time to get the information we needed out of the prisoner. Now it looks as if we'll have to take the bloodbeard along with us. We'll leave the older squires and enough men here to hold Camelot. Cynric and his Saxons should be able to deal with any threat to our boundaries in the meantime. Use the rest of today to polish your swords and say your goodbyes. We ride out tomorrow at first light."

The hall filled with noise as the knights began to discuss the campaign in excited voices.

Guinevere still looked worried. Sir Lancelot reached across to squeeze the queen's hand and told her not to open the gates until he got back. Cai was grinning from ear to ear. Rhianna smiled and slipped the black jewel back into her pocket.

Dragonland, she thought. *We're going to Dragonland tomorrow!*

⚜

The meeting broke up soon after that. Cai slid out of his chair and rushed around the table to Rhianna, his eyes shining with excitement.

"That was great!" he said. "It's going to be a proper war party, just like in King Arthur's day! Do you think they'll let me have a bigger horse to ride? Sandy's getting too small, really, now I've got a lance to carry. Will you ask the stablemaster to find a new mount for me? He'll listen to you…"

While the boy chattered on, a guard came in and muttered something to Sir Bors. The big knight exchanged a dark glance with Sir

Agravaine, and the pair of them hurried from the hall.

"Come on," Rhianna said. "I want to see what they're up to."

Her mother broke off her conversation with Sir Lancelot. "Darling, where are you going? I want to talk to you before you leave. I thought we could have lunch together…"

"Later, Mother! " she called back. "I've got to have a bath first."

The queen frowned after her as she and Cai escaped the hall.

Giggling, they ran down the long corridors after the two knights. "You shouldn't lie to your mother," Cai said. "A bath? That's a good one."

"Actually, I do have a bath waiting for me." Rhianna thought guiltily of Arianrhod, waiting up in the royal bathroom with the scented soaps, and lunch.

"Yeah, you do stink a bit," Cai said.

"So do you, *Sir* Cai!" She pushed him into the wall, and he gave her another grin.

"Watch it, Pendragon!" he teased. "Don't forget I carry the Lance of Truth now."

"Don't forget *I* carry the Sword of Light and can call on your knightly spirit to die for me any time I like." She rested her hand on the sword's hilt, but did not call on the magic. Excalibur was too powerful to use in play.

Cai sobered. "Is it true what you said about that pendant you wear being one of the jewels from King Arthur's crown?"

"Merlin says so. It hides my father's secrets, apparently. He doesn't know what they are, though."

The boy pulled a face. "More trouble, I expect. And now we're going to Dragonland, which is supposed to hide the gate to Annwn. I just hope Mordred's not found that! His bloodbeards are bad enough, without having the dead on his side as well."

Rhianna frowned, thinking uneasily of Mordred's witch-mother. "I thought the dead couldn't come back from Annwn? I thought only dead heroes who are taken to Avalon can return to the land of men, like the ones who ride with the Wild Hunt?" *Like my father will, when I take him the four Lights and his soul returns to his body*, she added silently.

"I dunno, Damsel Rhianna. The squires say the dead haunt the abandoned dragon lairs, and that's why it's so wild there. Nobody really knows what lives in Dragonland. Sir Lancelot

121

said all the dragons were dead, and we know *that's* not true…"

"Shh!" Rhianna said. "Hear that?"

Sir Bors and Sir Agravaine had turned down the steps leading into the dungeons. Torchlight flickered below, and they heard a faint scream. The sound was swallowed by stone and darkness, but the back of Rhianna's neck prickled.

She drew Excalibur and crept down the steps after the knights. Cai followed, his dagger clutched in his fist, treading on her skirt. The door at the bottom stood open. Beyond it lay darkness.

As they hesitated, a shadow loomed up the wall. A slender figure appeared in the doorway below, struggling to free her arm from Sir Agravaine's grip.

Rhianna's heart jumped in recognition. "It's

Arianrhod!" she said. "What's she doing down here? I told her to stay in my room. Come on!"

She leaped down the rest of the steps with Cai clattering at her heels and ran smack into Sir Bors, who stood guard at the bottom.

He whirled, his sword half out of its scabbard. "Damsel Rhianna!" he growled in exasperation. "Haven't I taught you never to creep up on an armed man like that? I might've killed you!"

"Where's Sir Agravaine taking Arianrhod?" Rhianna demanded. "She's innocent! She shouldn't be down here with the prisoners."

"Too right she shouldn't," Sir Bors said. "Bring her over here, Agravaine."

The dark-haired knight dragged the weeping Arianrhod across to them. The maid's eyes lit up in relief when she saw Rhianna.

She raised her tear-streaked face and said, "My lady, please tell them! I dozed off while I was waiting for you and had another dream, and when I woke up I was down here…"

"She brought food for that bloodbeard scum," Sir Agravaine growled. "I told the guards nothing to eat till I said, so they stopped her at the door and sent for us."

"It's cruel not to feed him," Arianrhod whispered.

"Are you crazy?" Cai said to her. "That man almost killed me out there yesterday, and now you're *feeding* him? Maybe you really are a spy for Prince Mordred, like everyone says you are."

"That's enough, Cai," Sir Bors grunted.

Arianrhod shook her head miserably. "No! I'm not a spy, I promise! Lady Rhianna, tell them, please."

Rhianna frowned at the maid, who cast nervous glances at something in Sir Agravaine's other hand that reflected the torchlight. With a chill, she recognised the dark mirror she'd stolen from Mordred in the summer – the one that worked as a spirit channel and they'd all assumed Mordred took with him when he escaped. Morgan Le Fay used it for her enchantments. Now she knew why her friend had been acting so strangely.

Mocking laughter came from the cells. "Throw the girl in here with me!" shouted the bloodbeard. "I'll soon teach her a lesson."

The guards went off to silence him.

"Why did you hide this mirror, Arianrhod?" Rhianna asked, taking the thing from Sir Agravaine and warily turning the glass to the wall.

The girl hung her head and whispered, "Lady Morgan came to me in a dream and told me to… I think I must have sleepwalked, as I don't remember hiding it."

"Did she tell you to take my pendant in the chapel, too?"

Arianrhod flushed. "I… don't remember."

Sir Bors sighed. "We haven't time to get to the bottom of this now. We've got work to do." He opened an empty cell door and checked inside. "Lock the maid in here for now. That'll keep her out of mischief till we're gone. We can't afford to lose the bloodbeard like we lost Mordred. We need him to lead us to his master."

"No!" Arianrhod gasped, and began to struggle afresh. "Please, my lady! Please don't let them put me in there!"

Rhianna stiffened. "It's not Arianrhod's

fault. She's under an enchantment."

"All the more reason to lock her up for her own safety," Sir Bors said gruffly. But his expression softened when Arianrhod started to cry. He called to one of the hovering guards. "Get the girl a proper bed down here, and whatever else she needs. She's to be treated well, but she's to be kept under guard till we're back from Dragonland."

The big knight frowned at Rhianna's blade. "Damsel Rhianna, be sensible and put that sword away before you hurt someone. I don't want a stupid fight over this. If you want to ride with us tomorrow, you'll let us deal with your maid the way we think best. Otherwise, we'll have to waste time sorting out the matter before we leave, and then Mordred might get hold of this crown that you and Merlin seem to want so much. So which is it to be?"

Rhianna clenched her fist, but slid Excalibur back into its scabbard. Sir Agravaine gave her friend a gentle push into the cell.

Arianrhod stared at them, tears running down both cheeks. "I got your bath ready before I fell asleep, my lady," she whispered. "But who's going to wash your hair for you?"

"I'll manage," Rhianna said brightly. "It doesn't have to be perfect. We're riding to war tomorrow, not a feast."

Cai drew himself up and said, "Yeah, Dragonland's no place for a damsel! You'll be much safer in here, Arianrhod."

The men glanced at Rhianna. She didn't know whether to laugh, or thump Cai for suggesting she wasn't a proper damsel.

"Cai," Sir Agravaine growled, propelling

the boy back up the steps. "I said, shut it."

Before the door closed on her friend's tearful face, Rhianna tightened her grip on the dark mirror. "No one will hurt you in here, Arianrhod," she promised. "I'll come and see you before we go tomorrow."

※

It was actually a relief not to have Arianrhod fussing over every little thing. After she'd bathed and eaten, Rhianna packed her own clothes, leaving out the tiaras and spare dresses her maid would have tried to include for her. Then she barred the door and propped the dark mirror on the windowsill.

She rummaged in her clothing chest and found another chain for the pendant – a stronger one than last time. She hung it around her neck and changed her slippers for her boots. Finally she drew Excalibur and stared into the black glass.

"Mordred!" she called. "I know you can hear me! The knights have got your bloodbeard spy locked in the dungeons. Arianrhod's safe. You'll never hurt her again."

At first, all she could see was her own reflection with Excalibur's blade glimmering in her hand. But as she peered closer, a shadow stirred in the glass. Quickly, she reversed Excalibur and brought the hilt of the sword down hard on the mirror.

There was a loud CRACK, and the glass shattered with an unexpected flash of green light.

Rhianna jumped out of range as the pieces tinkled to the floor. She smiled grimly and stamped on the broken glass to make sure all the magic was destroyed. It crunched satisfyingly under her boots, and the green light died.

She checked Excalibur, a bit worried the sword might have been harmed by the blow. But the Sword of Light had been forged in Avalon and seemed fine.

She laughed. "That scared you, didn't it, cousin?" she said to the empty room. "That's what happens when you come after my friends! You'd better start running, because we know where you are now, and we're coming after *you*!"

Dark Plans

Mordred woke in the shadrake's lair, bathed in sweat. What a nightmare! His cousin Rhianna had been standing over him with Excalibur, wearing the missing jewel from the Crown of Dreams around her neck. He'd woken up just as she brought the sword down to crush his skull.

He checked the crown was safe and scowled about the cave. His men had stabled the horses in one of the tunnels behind the waterfall and built a fire at the entrance. They had furnished this alcove for him from the dragon's treasure, but his captain should have

been back by now. How long did it take to
ride to Camelot and get a jewel off a silly
maid? It would be winter soon, and then
the rain would turn to snow. He shuddered
at the thought of being trapped in such a
godforsaken place until spring.

The crown glittered in the candlelight,
mocking him. So pretty, and yet so useless –
its jewels hiding magic he dared not use.
He snatched it up, limped over to his mother's
body and prodded her blackened bones with
a spear.

"Well?" he snapped. "What's happened to
my captain? Did he get into Camelot? Why's
he taking so long?"

The witch's spirit did not appear
immediately. Mordred ground his teeth in
frustration and raised the crown over his head.

"Mother!" he hissed. "If you don't answer me, I'll ride to Camelot right now and use this thing to claim the throne—"

"Not until you've taken care of Arthur's jewel, foolish boy!" the witch said, rippling into view at last and frowning at him. "Yes, your man is inside Camelot, but he seems to have got himself arrested. That interfering squire who carries the Lance of Truth saw through his disguise and challeged him to a duel. Unfortunately, my ex-maid wasn't able to get hold of the stone in time, and now it looks as if she won't be able to."

"What do you mean, woman? I thought you said you could control her?"

"I did what I could, but the girl was careless, and Rhianna smashed my mirror. Your cousin wears the jewel around her neck, and now it seems she's riding to Dragonland with the knights on a quest for the Crown. The bloodbeard must have talked."

Mordred frowned, thinking of his nightmare. "My men never talk under interrogation. They've all sworn to die first."

The witch gave a dark smile. "I'm sure they have. But a dead captain is no help to anyone. Alive, he might still be of some use to us. Don't worry, my son, all is not lost. Since we've failed to get the jewel out of Camelot, we'll let our eager Rhianna bring it to us."

"How many men are coming with her?" Mordred asked, getting worried now.

"I'm not sure. I've lost contact with my maid now. But I doubt all the knights will come. Lancelot will be too worried about leaving the queen unprotected, after we captured her up in the North last year. We just need to make sure our brave princess is separated from her friends so your man can get hold of the stone."

He smiled, feeling a bit better. "I'll make her give me the Sword of Light and the Lance of Truth as well," he said. "She's bound to bring them on her quest, isn't she?"

"That's my boy," the witch said. "But don't underestimate her this time! She almost got you killed in the summer. I'll do what I can to help, but I can't work miracles if you find yourself at the wrong end of her blade again. I think it's time you had a few lessons in using that crown of yours."

Mordred grinned, then remembered how she'd told him the crown had killed her. He eyed her blackened body. "I thought you said it was dangerous?"

"All magic is dangerous!" his mother snapped. "But your men won't stand a chance against two of the Lights unless you help them. A dragon attack should do it, and the Jewel of Annwn is strong in this place. I'll teach you all I know."

5
The Road to Dragonland

Arthur's knights rode out at first light
With Sword and Lance both shining bright,
To hunt the traitor who killed their king
In valleys shadowed by the dragon's wing.

Rhianna thought she'd never sleep. Pieces of the broken mirror flashed darkly at her from the floor every time she tried to close her eyes, reminding her of the way Morgan Le Fay had enchanted her friend. When she eventually dozed off, she dreamed of her cousin Mordred sitting in her father's place at the Round Table wearing the Crown of Dreams, and spent the rest of the night tossing and turning in a nightmare where the dark knight ruled Camelot.

She woke before dawn, dragged on her armour over her Avalonian leggings and laced up her boots. The yard was already full of horses and squires making ready for the journey. Shaking away the echoes of her dream, she buckled Excalibur around her waist with cold fingers. She reached for her father's black jewel and held it up to the light. Was it her imagination, or had it turned paler overnight?

She tucked the pendant under her armour and hurried downstairs to keep her promise to her friend.

The knights had already hauled their prisoner out of the dungeons. The bloodbeard stood shivering in the dawn, leashed by his wrists to the back of a wagon and watched by two armed guards. He looked tired and beaten. But when he spotted Rhianna crossing the yard, he raised his head and bared his teeth at her.

She glared back at him and hoped the knights would make him walk all the way to Dragonland.

The dungeons were deserted apart from Squire Gareth, who had been given the job of looking after Arianrhod. Her friend seemed to be the only one in the cells, which made her glad. At least the place wouldn't smell.

Gareth scowled when he saw her. "What are you doing down here? I thought you were riding to Dragonland with your *champion*, playing at knights."

"I want to see Arianrhod," she said.

The boy hesitated and glanced up the steps.

"Oh come on!" Rhianna snapped. "She's my friend. You know she's only locked down here for her own safety."

"She's a witch," Gareth muttered. "Sir Lancelot says she might put a spell on you."

"You don't really believe that! Let me in and I'll make sure you get guard duty on the walls instead of down here while we're gone."

He gave her a quick, hopeful look, then shrugged. "Don't matter to me. Won't be much excitement around these parts while you're away, any rate. Waste of time you all going after Mordred, if you ask me… you'll never find him if he doesn't want to be found."

"We're not just going to look for Mordred. I'm going to look for my father's crown, the one the dragon stole from the battlefield. The one that makes its wearer into the Pendragon."

That shut the boy up. He stared at her then shook his head. "So you fancy yourself as queen? Your mother might have something to say about that."

Rhianna sighed. "My mother knows why I'm going. Just let me in."

She waited until Gareth had closed the cell door behind her. Then she fumbled under her armour for the pendant. "Listen, Arianrhod..."

"Oh Lady Rhia!" The girl flung herself at her and held on tight. "My lady, please, you have to listen to me. You can't trust that bloodbeard! Last night, after you'd gone, there was a sharp pain in my head and I suddenly started remembering things. I know now why Lady Morgan made me come down here with her dark mirror – the bloodbeard used it to speak to her spirit! You've got to warn the knights. I think he's up to something."

Rhianna frowned. "I must have broken the enchantment when I smashed the mirror…"

"You smashed it?" Arianrhod blinked at her. "Then that must be why I remembered!"

Rhianna nodded grimly. "I didn't realise breaking it would cause you pain. Don't worry, nobody will be using that mirror to enchant anyone ever again. Listen, Arianrhod, this is more important. I want you to do something for me while we're away."

"I'll do anything for you, my lady, you know that!" the girl sniffed. "But how can I, if I'm locked up down here? I can't even clean your room for you. I'm not much use as a maid, am I?"

"You can do this."

Rhianna peeped through the door to check Gareth was not listening. She drew Arianrhod to the back of the cell and pulled the black jewel over her head. She hung it around the girl's slender neck. "I want you to look after this while I'm away," she whispered. "Try not to let anybody see it. If they do, just say it's an old pendant I gave to you because I didn't like it, all right?"

Arianrhod's eyes widened as she touched the stone. "My lady! But this is your father's jewel—"

"Yes, and I think it'll be safer with you in here until we get back. Just in case that bloodbeard is up to something, as you say.

Nobody must know you've got it."

The girl smiled. "Don't you worry, Lady Rhia. I'll guard it with my life!"

Rhianna smiled too. "You won't need to do that. Gareth is supposed to guard you with *his* life. As long as none of Mordred's bloodbeards get down here while we're gone, it should be safe enough. If Lady Isabel comes to see you, just tell her what I told you. With all the knights gone to Dragonland, my mother's the only one who's likely to recognise the pendant, and I doubt she'll come down to the cells."

Arianrhod sighed. "No, the queen never visits the dungeons. She's been afraid of the dark ever since Mordred captured her and locked her up in his tower." She glanced uneasily at the shadows.

Rhianna hadn't known that. Her mother hid it well.

"Have you got everything you need in here?" she asked.

Now that it had a proper bed and rugs on the floor, the cell looked much more comfortable than yesterday. Arianrhod had taken one of the bedcovers and fixed it to the hooks on the wall, so it hung like a tapestry. She had been allowed some candles too, spare dresses, and her trinket box full of Rhianna's unwanted jewellery.

Arianrhod nodded. "I've enough, my lady."

"Good." Rhianna gave her an awkward hug and knocked on the door. When Gareth let her out, she looked back at her friend and hesitated. "Will you be all right?"

Arianrhod sat on the edge of the bed and gave Rhianna a brave smile. "It's not for long, is it?

You'll soon be back with the Crown of Dreams."

Rhianna smiled too. "As soon as I can, I promise."

"And then the knights will kill Mordred, so we can all be safe."

"Yes," Rhianna said, trying not to think too much about her cousin. "And when I've found the Crown, we can all go and look for the Grail of Stars and bring King Arthur back from Avalon. Then nobody will hurt you or lock you up in a dungeon ever again, I promise."

Gareth rolled his eyes.

Arianrhod bit her lip. She started to say something else, but Cai's voice yelled from above, "Damsel Rhianna? Are you still down there? Sir Bors says if you're not up here in two shakes of a horse's tail, we're leaving without you!"

"Go, my lady!" her friend said. "And don't forget your hairbrush…"

"It's already packed!" Rhianna lied, grinning as she sprang up the steps.

❈

They took the Roman road the knights had used when they rode to the North Wall in the spring to rescue the queen and bring back Sir Lancelot. As they crossed the bridge, Rhianna looked back at Camelot's white towers and remembered how she had watched the knights ride out that day, as much a prisoner in her room as Arianrhod was now, in the dungeon. But she'd got out with a bit of help from her friends.

She patted Alba's shining neck. "The knights know that even if they locked me in the dungeon, I'd find a way to escape and follow them," she told the mare.

Alba tossed her head. *I want to gallop*, she complained. *These big horses are very slow.*

Rhianna smiled. "I know they are, my darling," she said. "But at least we're going with them this time. That's more fun than using the druid path to catch up with them, isn't it?"

Elphin glanced at her and shook his head. No doubt he'd have preferred to use the magical path Merlin had shown them, which allowed them to travel quickly between stone circles using the spiral pathfinder Elphin wore around his neck to open the mists. But she always found riding with the knights exciting.

The men were in high spirits because Sir Lancelot led them again. The big horses pranced, the knights' lances glittered in the sun, and her father's red and gold dragon banner flapped proudly in the breeze. People ran out of the villages and towns to wave and cheer as they trotted past. Rhianna didn't even mind that they wouldn't let her ride at the front. Here, in the middle of the party with her friends, she could keep an eye on the bloodbeard, who stumbled along behind the wagon. He seemed docile enough, but she didn't want him behind her where he might get up to mischief.

She checked the sky for Merlin, but couldn't see the little falcon. Before leaving the castle, the knights had sent messages by hawk to the volunteers who manned the druid beacons which formed a line of sight across the Summer Sea, from Camelot to an old fortress on the far shore. Merlin had flown off with the hawks to check the fire magic would still work if the volunteers needed it. He'd promised to meet them in Dragonland. She just hoped he wouldn't get distracted by a rabbit and forget.

As they rode further north, Elphin gazed across the marshes beside the road, humming a sad song in his throat. The raised banks and stretches of misty water suddenly seemed familiar.

"Isn't that the way to Avalon?" she said, remembering how they had ridden in the opposite direction with Sir Bors and Sir Agravaine last year, after losing Merlin in the mists between worlds. So long ago, it seemed now.

Her friend nodded. "I think so, yes."

"Then aren't we going the wrong way? I thought Dragonland was back that way. Oh, Arianrhod *said* that bloodbeard was up to something! We've got to warn the knights."

"We can't cross the Summer Sea with all these horses, Damsel Rhianna," Cai said. "They don't have magic shoes like your mist horses do. We got to keep going north on this road till we get to Corinium, and then head west across the river to Dragonland."

"How long will that take?" Rhianna looked longingly at the narrow tracks leading off into the mist. "Elphin, you don't think we could...?"

He put a hand on her rein. "No, Rhia," he said firmly. "Let's find out where Mordred's hiding first."

They camped that night on a hill near a town with public baths built by the Romans. Rhianna wanted to visit them, but Sir Bors wouldn't hear of it. "This isn't a sightseeing trip, Damsel Rhianna," he reminded her, tweaking her braid. "Besides, you had a bath last night, didn't you? Two baths in two days is a bit much for someone who grew up in Avalon. I thought you'd at least want to roll in some mud first."

Rhianna flushed as the other knights chuckled. She caught the bloodbeard looking at her again and scowled at him.

They passed through Corinium without stopping and headed west. This road was more overgrown and showed fewer prints. They trotted past some blackened, smoking huts and then came to a town beside a river, where the people did not cheer them. When they saw the Pendragon banner, they complained about a dragon swooping out of the hills and setting fire to their homes.

Sir Agravaine went to question them and came back looking grave.

"It can't be the shadrake that attacked us last year," he said uneasily. "Unless it's learned to breathe fire as well as ice. We're getting close to the border. If this is Mordred's doing, we'll have to keep a good lookout from here on in."

Sir Bors rode his horse across to the bloodbeard and seized his hair in one fist. "You know anything about this?" he growled.

The prisoner bared his teeth. "Ask the damsel," he said. "She's a Pendragon, isn't she? Meant to be able to control dragons, I've heard. Maybe she sent the beast?"

"You know that's a lie!" Rhianna clenched her hand on Excalibur's hilt and glared at the bloodbeard.

"Don't, Rhia," Elphin whispered, putting

his hand over hers. "He's only trying to upset you. Stay away from him."

She was glad when they left the burning town behind. She felt sorry for its people, but the knights didn't have time to stop and help them. The road got rougher as they rode. The mist horses delicately picked their way over the stones and puddles, but the bigger horses stumbled, and the wagon wheels kept getting stuck in the mud. Wooded valleys dripping with wet ferns led off between the hills. They went slower and slower as the road became little more than a sheep track. Rhianna divided her attention between the hills and the trees, keeping an eye out for dragons and worrying about Merlin.

As she was wondering how they would ever find her cousin or the Crown of Dreams in such a wild land, shouts came from the front of the party, and the wagon carrying their supplies jerked to yet another stop.

"It's that bloodbeard again," Elphin said.

Cai stood in his stirrups to see, and almost dropped his lance when Sandy put a hoof down a pothole.

"He's sat down in the mud," Cai reported. "Sir Bors is trying to make him get up. Dunno why he's bothering. They should just drag him if he refuses to walk."

Rhianna frowned. "Cai, stop showing off," she said. "Don't forget that's the Lance of Truth you're carrying, not a squire's spear."

Cai pulled a face. "It might as well be! The knights still treat me like a squire. They seem to have forgotten I was the one who challenged that spy to a duel and lured him into their trap so they could catch him."

"They haven't forgotten you fell off, though," Elphin said, winking at Rhianna.

"I wouldn't have done if Damsel Rhia hadn't got in the way," Cai grumbled. "I'd have unhorsed that bloodbeard. I'm supposed to be her champion. She should have let me take care of it. Tell her, Elphin."

"I tried," Elphin said, still teasing. "You know she never listens when she's got a sword in her hand."

Before Rhianna could argue, Sir Bedivere came trotting back down the column. "Cai, get down off that pony," he called. "We need something for the prisoner to ride that won't get him very far if he makes a run for it. This road's not made for carts. We're going to leave the wagon here and carry the supplies between us."

Cai frowned at the bloodbeard. "But what about me?"

Rhianna saw the men unhitch the horses from the wagon and smiled in understanding. "You wanted a bigger horse, didn't you Cai?"

"You can take one of the carthorses, Cai," Sir Bedivere confirmed. "That grey mare's quiet enough."

Cai's face broke into a grin. He patted the pony apologetically. "I'm sorry, Sandy. I'll come and groom you tonight."

While Cai struggled on to the back of the tall dappled mare, the knights hauled the bloodbeard into Sandy's saddle and linked his ankles under the pony's belly with the rope. They passed Sandy's reins to Sir Bors. The bloodbeard sat silently and sulked.

"He hoped they'd untie him so he could

make a break for the hills," Elphin said.

Rhianna watched the unloading of the wagon impatiently, itching to make a break for the hills herself. Then Cai barged between them on his big mare. Alba shook her mane and made a comment about human boys who could not control their horses.

They made better progress after that, though still too slow for Rhianna's liking. In the afternoon, it started to rain. She pulled her cloak over her head and thought how pointless a hairbrush would have been.

❧

That night, they camped in a wooded valley with a loud stream rushing down a gully. The bloodbeard was hauled off his pony and leashed to a tree as usual. Cai went to comfort

Sandy, while Elphin took Evenstar for a drink. As Rhianna unsaddled Alba, she felt the bloodbeard watching her again. She scowled at him.

"You," he hissed. "Yes, you, Pendragon girl! Come over here. I've got something to tell you."

She glanced around. Nobody else had heard. His guards were struggling to erect a shelter in the rain and wind. The knights were still seeing to their horses and trying to light a fire so they could cook supper. Sentries patrolled the edges of the camp, keeping a lookout for enemies in the dark.

"Don't be scared," the bloodbeard said, raising his bound wrists. "What can I do, trussed up like this? I've been trying to talk to you for ages. But them knights of yours keep you wrapped up like a soft damsel who's afraid of getting a twig stuck in her hair."

This got Rhianna's blood up. Clenching her fist on Excalibur, she strode across. But even though he seemed docile enough, she remembered Arianrhod's warning and stood carefully out of reach. "What do you want?" she said.

He glanced at his guards, who cursed the shelter as a sudden gust of wind ripped it from its ties to collapse on their heads. "Come closer, Pendragon girl," he whispered.

She wasn't going to fall for that trick. "I can hear you just fine from here."

The bloodbeard pulled a face. "Please yourself. But my information isn't for anybody else's ears. It concerns your father's crown."

Rhianna's skin prickled. She glanced back at Elphin and Cai, who were still grooming the horses. "What do you know about King Arthur's crown?" she said. "Have you seen it?"

"Oh, I've seen it all right." The bloodbeard grimaced. "Want to know where, don't you Pendragon maid? Got your eye on it yourself, no doubt? Mighty pretty it is too, with all those jewels. Suit you very well, I'd say."

She saw one of the knights glance in their direction, and crouched behind a bush so her bright hair wouldn't give her away. "If you tell me where you saw it, I'll see if I can get you something hot to eat tonight," she whispered.

The bloodbeard's face twisted a bit, and she knew she'd touched a nerve. "I'm not hungry," he grunted. "We northerners are used to fighting on empty bellies, unlike you soft summer landers."

"Please yourself," Rhianna said. She eyed

his leash. It looked too short to allow him much movement. She crept behind his tree and quietly drew Excalibur. With a quick leap, she put the blade to the bloodbeard's throat. "Now tell!" she said.

He grinned at her. "Nice move. But I think you're bluffing, Pendragon maid. I've heard you can't blood that sword of yours if you want to take it back to Avalon for your father."

"Maybe I don't want to give it to my father. Maybe I want to keep it for myself. So tell me where you saw the Crown of Dreams! Quick, before the knights come back. I'll count to three. One… two…" She pushed the sword a little harder against his throat.

He pressed his head back against the tree and laughed softly. "All right, all right! You'd do a better job of interrogation than your knights, I'm thinking. But if you cut my throat, you'll never find your father's crown, because I'm the only one who can lead you to it. It's in a dragon's lair quite close to here. If you release me, I'll take you there."

"Why are you helping me?" Rhianna asked, suspicious.

"Prince Mordred abandoned me. He sent me to Camelot alone to punish me for letting him get captured in the summer, knowing I'd be caught and tortured. If I help you gain the crown, you'll keep Mordred off the throne and I'll be safe from his revenge. If you want to kill me afterwards that's up to you, but I prefer to put my trust in Arthur's daughter than in Morgan Le Fay's witch-brat."

She stepped towards him, lowering Excalibur. "Where?" she demanded. "Where is this dragon's lair? Is Mordred there, too?"

"Funnily enough, that's just what your bullies of knights want to know."

He suddenly lunged forward and grabbed her ankle. She stumbled in surprise as the leash uncoiled from where he'd been hiding it under some leaves and looped around her arm. He slammed her wrist against the tree, sending the sword flying. His hands grabbed her hair, catching in the tangles, and she felt his filthy fingers fumbling at her throat.

It was a trick, after all.

"You're lying!" she choked, trying to free herself but only getting more tangled in the rope. "You've no idea where the Crown is. You just want to escape… so you can run… back to your master… let me *go*!"

◀◖ 6 ◗▶

Ambush

Arthur's great army fought on the plain
But their horses stumbled in the rain.
Attacked by dragons, their blood ran red
In mist-bound valley their captive fled.

The sound of their struggle alerted
the knights. Help came in a confusion
of shouts and running feet. Cai, who was
closest, charged across the clearing with the
Lance of Truth and launched it at Rhianna's

attacker with a furious yell.

She fought to free her hair from the bloodbeard's grasp as he hauled her in front of him to make a human shield. "No, Cai!" she gasped.

Fortunately, the boy missed his target in the dark. The lance sparkled past Rhianna's ear and got stuck in the tree. While Cai struggled to free it, Elphin's harp tinkled out into the night, distracting the bloodbeard. Sir Bors and Sir Agravaine came running with Sir Bedivere hot on their heels, shouting at the prisoner's guards to help.

The men struggled out of their collapsed shelter. They grabbed the bloodbeard and hauled him back against the trunk, wrapping his leash around his neck until he half choked.

Sir Bedivere helped Rhianna up, while

Sir Bors thumped the prisoner on the nose. The bloodbeard grinned and spat blood into the big knight's face, so Sir Bors thumped him again.

Sir Lancelot arrived and took charge with a furious glare. "What's going on here? Get the princess away from that man! I promised Queen Guinevere I wouldn't let him get within spitting distance of her!" He scowled at the two guards. "How did this happen? What were you two doing while the prisoner was attacking our princess?"

The men flushed and mumbled something about the shelter falling on them.

Sir Bedivere took Rhianna's elbow and tried to lead her away. She pulled free of him and picked up Excalibur. She looked down at the bloodbeard, panting, and gripped the hilt of her sword. She wanted to punish him for tricking her but couldn't get past Sir Bors, who seemed intent on beating the prisoner to death.

Then Elphin's music *changed*, and she began to think more clearly. She raised Excalibur until its blade gleamed in the firelight and shouted, "Stop!"

The big knight stepped back. Cai, who had finally managed to free the Lance of Truth from the tree, came to stand beside her. He pointed the lance at the bloodbeard.

"Don't kill him," Rhianna said. "He didn't hurt me, not really. It was my fault. I was stupid, I got too close."

Sir Lancelot frowned at her. "You sure you're all right, Princess?"

"Yes. I didn't see him down there in the dark, and he... er... caught my ankle as

I went past." She saw the bloodbeard's eyes flicker to her face and dared him to say more. "We need him to show us where Mordred's hiding, don't we?" she said. "He won't be able to do that if you strangle him."

At this, the guards loosened the rope from the prisoner's throat. The bloodbeard coughed and sagged in relief, gasping for air.

Sir Lancelot sighed. "Princess Rhianna's right," he said. "Secure that man so he can't move, and don't take your eyes off him from now on. If you know what's good for you, you'll not try that again!" he added to the prisoner. "You've just said goodbye to your supper. We don't feed scum like you who think it's funny to attack defenceless damsels in the dark."

"I'm not a defenceless damsel," Rhianna pointed out.

But the knights were not listening.

"Serves you jolly well right if you starve to death!" Cai said, giving the bloodbeard a jab with the Lance of Truth before they left him to his guards.

Rhianna discovered she was shaking. It took her three attempts to sheathe Excalibur. She clenched her teeth, still angry with herself for being fooled by the bloodbeard's lies.

❦

"Why did you go over to talk to him?" Elphin whispered later, as they sat beside the fire sharing some nuts and berries, while the men chewed strips of salty journey meat.

"She didn't," Cai said with his mouth full. "You heard her. He tripped her up in the dark, the sneak. Probably been looking for a chance to get his greasy hands on her ever since we left Camelot. Are you *sure* you're not hurt, Damsel Rhianna? He looked like he was trying to strangle you! Good thing we stopped him in time."

She rubbed her throat and frowned. "I don't think he wanted to kill me. I think he was looking for something."

Elphin's gaze flew to her neck. "King Arthur's jewel? Is it still safe?"

"I hope so," Rhianna said, thinking of Arianrhod locked in Camelot's dungeon.

Cai frowned. "What do you mean, you hope so? Can't you check?"

"She can't check, because she hasn't brought it with her," Elphin said quietly. "Have you, Rhia?"

Her friend's violet eyes held hers, full of the magic of Avalon. She couldn't lie to him, even if she wanted to. "No," she admitted with a sigh. "I left the jewel with Arianrhod."

"You did *what*?" Cai jumped to his feet. "But that's no good! I thought we're supposed to put it back into the crown when we find it, so that its magic will work properly?"

"Sit down, Cai," Elphin said, still quietly. "Don't tell the whole world." He glanced across at the prisoner's tree to check the bloodbeard wasn't listening. "So now he knows you haven't got the jewel."

"He knows I'm not wearing it. He doesn't know we haven't brought it with us in one of our packs."

Elphin nodded. "Good point. You might be right about it being safer where it is, if Mordred's lurking around these parts as well. I don't like the sound of those dragons burning towns. But you still haven't told us why you went to talk to that bloodbeard captain in the first place."

"She didn't—" Cai began.

"I wanted to find out more about King Arthur's crown," Rhianna admitted. She told the others how the bloodbeard claimed to have seen it. "But he's lying, isn't he? He obviously only said that to lure me close enough for him to grab me so he could steal the jewel and take it to his master."

"Yeah," said Cai. "He must be lying, because whoever wears that crown becomes the next king of Camelot, and we all know that's not going to be Prince Mordred."

Elphin said nothing. They looked at the tree again, where the prisoner was slumped in his tight bonds. He'd have a stiff neck in the morning. Rhianna wished she'd had time to ask him more questions before he'd grabbed her. Could she creep over there when the others were asleep?

"Don't even think about it, Rhia," Elphin whispered, guessing her thoughts. "I played the sleeping magic for him. He'll be dead to the world until we're ready to ride in the morning."

※

Morning dawned grey and damp. While she saddled Alba, Rhianna fretted about Merlin. How would the druid ever find them in these foggy valleys? He was such a small hawk. What if he'd got lost or eaten by a dragon on his way across the Summer Sea? Then she fretted about the bloodbeard and his claim to have seen the Crown of Dreams. What if he hadn't been lying? What if he really did want to betray Mordred and help her? She needed to ask Merlin what to do, but as usual the druid was never around when she needed him.

Alba had to nudge her for attention. *You are very distracted this morning*, the mare snorted. *You put my bridle on backwards. It is hurting my ears.*

Rhianna stopped looking for the little hawk and patted her mist horse. "Oh! I'm sorry, my darling!"

She sorted out the bridle. Then she helped Cai mount his big grey mare and passed him the Lance of Truth, before vaulting into her own saddle. Elphin was already mounted on Evenstar. She watched the bloodbeard as the men hauled him on to the pony. In the daylight, she could see his new bruises.

One eye was swollen shut, and he seemed woozy, almost falling out of his saddle. His guards had to walk alongside to hold him on.

Elphin's enchantment must still be working, she supposed. She'd have to wait until later to get any sense out of him.

The track wound steeply upwards, and soon they were surrounded by thick mist. The knights had to ride in single file, and they lost sight of the front and the back of their party. Rhianna gave up hoping for the merlin to appear. If the druid was flying in this, then he could look after himself. Alba tucked her head to her chest in misery.

Just as she wondered if they had lost the road entirely, she glimpsed green lights in the mist. She squinted uneasily at them. The jewel on Excalibur's hilt began to glow.

"I don't like this, Rhia," Elpin whispered, reaching for his harp. "There's magic at work here…"

Even as he spoke, an unearthly shriek came out of the fog. They heard the flap of large wings overhead.

"Look out!" Cai yelled. "Dragons!"

Rhianna ducked as a monstrous, winged creature dived out of the clouds to strike the knight riding in front of them. He fell from his saddle with a grunt, and the dragon snatched up his dropped sword to add to its treasure pouch. The other knights spun their horses on the narrow path, drawing their swords as a second dragon swooped down on them.

Alba reared in terror, and Rhianna had to grab the mare's mane to stay on. She fumbled desperately for Excalibur and drew the shining blade, trying to see where the first creature had gone. Yells of alarm sounded ahead, and a riderless horse galloped past them.

Shouts and curses came from the back of the party as the loose horse reached them.

"What's happening?"

"Who fell off?"

"Is Merlin back?"

"That's no hawk, stupid! Don't you know a dragon when you see one?"

"One? There's hundreds of 'em up there! Look out…"

Rhianna tensed. She could only see two of the creatures. Then Sir Lancelot yelled back down the path, "Protect the princess!" and several big horses pressed close to Alba, blocking her view.

The second dragon made another dive at

the column, causing yet more panic and confusion. Seeing the shadow of its wings in the mist, she thought at first it was the shadrake that had attacked them in the summer. But then it opened its mouth and belched out flame, rather than ice, and she realised it must be one of the dragons that had burned the border town.

Elphin pulled out his harp. Avalonian music tinkled across the hillside, and the dragon-fire soon fizzled out. But the horses were terrified now, bucking and plunging and neighing. The knights had a hard time staying in their saddles.

The first dragon swooped back out of the smoke. Rhianna swung Excalibur at the creature as it passed overhead. It was so close she could feel the heat of its fiery breath on her cheek. Flames licked her hair. She beat them out with her shield and held on grimly to the sword, its blade shining in the mist.

"Leave us alone!" she yelled. "I am Rhianna Pendragon, and I order you to go home!"

Her voice sounded small compared to the dragons' shrieks, but they heard her.

"WE KNOW YOU ARE THE PENDRAGON MAID," boomed one.

"WE MUST NOT HARM YOU."

"BUT WE CAN TAKE ALL YOUR PRETTY WEAPONS."

"You won't take mine!" Cai yelled, raising the Lance of Truth. "This here's a magic lance, so you'd better watch out. Stay away from Damsel Rhianna, or I'll skewer you with it and roast you over your own fire." His new horse did not look so quiet any more, but he clung bravely to the reins as the grey mare pranced like a warhorse.

Alba pranced too, not to be outdone. *Do you want me to race Sandy again?* the mare asked.

Rhianna's head hurt with the booming dragon voices, and her right arm ached from swinging Excalibur over her head. For a moment she thought her mare was confused and had forgotten Cai no longer rode the pony. Then she saw Sandy's tail disappearing into the mist with their prisoner. In the confusion of the dragons' attack, the bloodbeard had somehow taken control of the reins with his bound hands.

"Sandy!" Cai wailed, noticing the escaped prisoner too.

Rhianna stared after the pony in frustration. "The bloodbeard's getting away!" she shouted at the knights. "I'll be all right – go after him!"

As the knights hesitated, the dragons dived again one from each side. Fire lit up the hillside, showing wild-eyed horses, confused men, and frightened squires clutching their weapons, not sure whether to fight or flee.

Cai's mare reared, and as he flung his arms around his horse's neck the Lance of Truth came whistling down across Alba's nose. The little horse misted to avoid it. Rhianna gave up trying to fight right-handed according to the knightly code, and swapped Excalibur back to her left hand. As she did so, a large claw appeared out of the smoke and struck her arm. The sword went spinning out of her grasp.

With a cry of triumph, the second dragon back-winged and snatched Excalibur out of the air. Weakness washed over Rhianna as the sword vanished into the dragon's pouch.

"THANK YOU, PENDRAGON MAID, THIS IS A VERY SHINY WEAPON. WE WILL GO NOW."

"It's taking the Sword of Light!" she shouted, dragging Alba's head around. She stood in her stirrups in a futile attempt to regain the sword. "Elphin, *do something*!"

Her friend raised his harp again, but the music did not have much effect on the dragon, which shrieked a final farewell as it flapped away into the mist. The other dragon swooped one last time and snatched up a few more dropped weapons before flying after its friend.

Elphin's fingers moved faster and faster as he tried to put out all the fires the creatures had started. Cai had somehow kept hold of the Lance, but had lost control of his reins. None of the knights were chasing the bloodbeard. They had scattered across the hillside, still fighting invisible dragons. She heard Lancelot's voice shouting orders from the mist, faint and far away.

"Over here!" Rhianna shouted. "They went that way! Can't you see?"

But the knights obviously couldn't see. And without Excalibur to light up the mist, she couldn't see very much, either. Was that shadow another dragon? Maybe the knights were right, and there were more of the creatures than she thought?

She hesitated a moment longer. The dragons would be weighed down by the weapons they had stolen from the knights, but they could still fly faster than any horse could gallop.

"Race that dragon, Alba!" She dug her heels into the little horse's sides.

The mare barged past the nearest knight's horse, almost knocking Rhianna out of the saddle. She saw the man's wide-eyed look. Then they were plunging off the path and down the rocky hillside after the dragon that had stolen her sword.

DARK TRAP

Mordred ripped the Crown from his head with a shaking hand. It burned his forehead every time he put it on. He dared not wear it for long periods.

Dragon wings still flapped in his ears, and he could hear the echo of their booming voices. He stared around the shadrake's lair in alarm. The knights had escaped the ambush and were coming this way! At the sight of his men dozing around the fire instead of keeping watch at the tunnel, his alarm turned to panic.

"Mother!" he yelled. "Mother, help me!"

The witch glimmered into view, looking

serene and beautiful in the glow of the green
jewel. She frowned at his trembling hand.
"Pull yourself together, boy!" she snapped.
"Don't drop that crown. What's wrong
this time?" Her voice turned sickly sweet,
taunting him. "Your cousin send you another
nightmare?"

"Worse," he reported, clutching the crown.
"She's coming down here!"

Woken by his yell, two breathless
bloodbeards appeared at his alcove, weapons
drawn. He waved them away with a scowl.
"I thought I told you to keep watch! Get
back to your posts. Can't you see I'm busy?"
The men took one look at his mother's spirit
and backed out again.

He lowered his voice. "I sent the dragons
to ambush the knights like you said, but

the stupid creatures won't obey me. They abandoned the attack, and now Rhianna's bringing Arthur's entire army to murder me! I thought you said they wouldn't all leave Camelot? Sir Lancelot's leading them and that bully Sir Bors is with them too. I'm sure I spotted Sir Agravaine and Bedivere as well... If they trap me down here, I'm dead."

The witch sighed. "Arthur was never such a coward, even before he wore the Crown. I suppose you've lost contact with the dragons?"

"Stupid things flew off with the Sword!"

"Excalibur?" the witch said, eyebrows raised.

"Of course Excalibur," Mordred said, rubbing his temples. "I wouldn't have given myself a splitting headache getting them to steal some ordinary sword. I've plenty of useless old blades down here already." He cast a scathing look around the piles of treasure.

His mother sighed again. "Didn't I warn you not to try anything tricky with that Crown until you've dealt with Arthur's jewel? Dragons are difficult enough to control, as it is."

"They were meant to bring the sword to me, not fly off with the thing," he muttered.

To his surprise, she chuckled. "Still, it was a good try. Without Excalibur, the girl will be vulnerable. She's coming this way, you say? Is she alone?"

Mordred calmed down a bit and started to think more clearly. "She was when I last saw her. But the knights won't be far behind."

The witch smiled. "Leave the knights to me. You concentrate on the damsel. Do you think you can handle her on your own, or do you need my help for that, too?"

Mordred brightened up at the thought of his cousin trapped in here with him. He put the crown back on and went to rouse his men. "Make yourselves useful and find a strong chain!" he told them. "Fix it to the wall over there. We're making this place ready for a princess."

7

Captive

The thief lured Rhianna from the hill
Through valleys where ancient
stones stand still
And enemies lurk in shadowed wood
To catch a damsel with their muffling hood.

Rhianna galloped blind into the mist.
She could not see much past her mare's
white ears and soon lost sight of the dragons.
She heard someone call her name and glanced

back to see Elphin urging Evenstar after her. Cai's horse followed him, the Lance of Truth swinging wildly.

Too embarrassed about losing her sword to face her friends yet, she urged Alba faster. They crossed a river, galloping over the surface of the water in a sparkle of Avalonian magic, raced up the hill on the other side and plunged into the next valley. Now she couldn't hear the dragons ahead or her friends behind.

Alba's neck foamed with sweat as she dodged through the trees. Rocks flashed under the mare's dainty hooves. Then a mossy stone loomed out of the mist right in front of them. Rhianna had been watching the sky, so did not see it in time to swerve. Alba threw up her head at the last moment and *misted*.

She grabbed desperately for the disappearing

mane, knowing she was going to fall off, just as she used to before she carried Excalibur. She prayed it would be a soft landing, and her head would not hit a rock. Trees and sky whirled around her as she rolled in wet leaves and came to a stop against another stone.

Still a bit shaky, she picked herself up and caught Alba's rein. She was furious with herself for losing Excalibur. Her friends could easily have been hurt by those dragons. Now she couldn't even protect them if the creatures attacked again, because she had lost the Sword of Light.

I am sorry I misted, Alba snorted. *Please do not be angry.*

"I'm not angry with you, silly," she said, patting the tired mare. "I should never have tried to swap sword hands back there, and

I didn't look where I was going again, did I? Who put that thing in such a stupid place, anyway?"

She scowled at the stone that had caused her fall. More mossy stones loomed out of the mist nearby, reminding her of the stone circle where they'd taken the magical spiral path north to catch up with the knights in the summer. But some of them leaned at strange angles, and others lay broken in the ferns.

She started to worry about her friends. What if they'd been hurt trying to keep up with her? Cai had the Lance of Truth to carry, and he wasn't that good a rider yet.

"Don't worry, my darling," she said to Alba, trying not to think about the dragons. "I expect they've stopped at that river. Cai's horse can't gallop across water."

Evenstar can gallop over the river, Alba reminded her.

"Elphin would stay to help Cai. We'll go back and find them, and then we'll look for that dragon together."

She began to lead the mare back the way they had come then stopped, her neck prickling. Ahead, a rider waited in the mist between the trunks. The horse looked about the right size for Cai's new mount, but its rider did not carry a lance. Had he dropped it?

"Cai?" she called, leading Alba towards the horse.

The rider turned his mount and trotted away into the trees.

"Cai, you idiot – it's me!"

She caught movement out of the corner of her eye and stopped again. Another horse trotted through the trees nearby.

"Elphin…?" she said, less sure now.

It is not Evenstar, her mare said.

Rhianna's stomach clenched. The knights looking for her, maybe? "Sir Bors?" she whispered. "Sir Bedivere? Is that you?"

The second rider raised a bow, and a black-feathered arrow thudded into the tree beside her.

Heart pounding, she vaulted back into her saddle and urged Alba into a gallop, ducking branches and swerving around trees. Her neck prickled as more arrows zipped past her ears. *I'm wearing my Avalonian armour*, she reminded herself. Then she remembered how the last time she'd been hit by a bloodbeard's arrow, before she'd got Excalibur out of the lake, she had fallen off. She fumbled for the

Pendragon shield that was strapped to her saddle and raised it over her head.

This meant she could not gallop so fast, but fortunately her attackers could not get a good aim through the trees, either. Then the air around her shimmered green, and the stones loomed back out of the trees – she must have ridden in a circle! As she slowed Alba, confused, the bushes in front of her erupted with dark shapes. Alba misted again, and she grabbed for the mane in desperation. She almost stayed on this time, but she still felt dizzy from her earlier fall and lost her balance.

She rolled at the feet of her assailants, while her mare galloped off. A sack went over her head. She struggled and kicked, but it did no good. There were at least four of them, and they were grown men, stronger than her. They took the shield, pinned her arms to her sides, and wound a rope around the outside of the sack.

"Damn little wildcat!" one said, sitting on her legs. "Near had my eye out. Get hold of that white pony of hers, before her friends come down here looking for her."

"Nah, they're too busy with those dragons."

"I only saw two of the beasts, and last I saw they was flapping off home. Prince Mordred's obviously not as in control of them as he thinks he is."

"Stop chattering and take her boots," snapped a new voice. With sinking heart, she recognised it as belonging to the bloodbeard captain who had escaped earlier. He bent down to whisper through the sack. "Time you found out what it feels like to be alone among enemies, Princess."

"Let me go!" she said, angry with herself for riding straight into his trap. "I'm King Arthur's daughter! His knights will hunt you down, and this time they'll kill you for sure. My friends are right behind me, they'll be here any moment... they've got the Lance of Truth... and Elphin's a prince of Avalon... he can do magic..."

She got a mouthful of sack as the bloodbeard pushed her head down into the leaves. He chuckled. "Then we'd better get you somewhere safe where they can't find you, hadn't we?"

Rhianna felt them tug off her boots. As the rope went around her ankles, she sucked in a final breath. "Find Evenstar, Alba!" she called through the muffling sack. She heard the thud of small hooves fading and went limp with relief. At least they hadn't caught her mist horse.

"Sorry, sir," one of the men muttered. "Crazy animal nearly trampled me."

"Let it go," grunted Rhianna's captor, hauling her up. "We can't waste time chasing it now. Nice and quiet, I said. You made enough noise to wake the dead."

"The dead *are* awake, sir," said one of the men in a nervous tone. "I'm sure I saw Mordred's witch-mother back in that lair."

"They're on our side, don't worry."

The captain chuckled and lifted Rhianna across a saddle. She started to kick again, then felt a pony's muzzle sniff her bare feet and realised it must be Sandy. She lay more quietly, glad of his familiar bulk beneath her.

"That's right, Princess," the bloodbeard said, mistaking her limpness for fear. "You lie nice and still and you won't get hurt. Prince

Mordred wants to talk to you about a jewel."

※

Prince Mordred wants to talk to you about a jewel.

All through that jolting, smothering ride, the bloodbeard's words churned in Rhianna's head. Did that mean Mordred had found the crown? If he had got hold of it, he would use it to attack Camelot, and without Excalibur she'd not be able to stop him.

At first she hung limply over Sandy's back, sick with worry for her friends, unable to think straight. Then she realised that if Mordred *had* found out how to use the crown's magic, he wouldn't need to talk to her. He'd simply have told his men to kill her. She remembered Merlin saying no impostor could take the throne while Arthur's jewel was safe, and breathed again inside the sack. Thank goodness she hadn't brought the pendant with her to Dragonland.

She tested the ropes again. But they were not going to come off in a hurry, and the bloodbeards had taken her boots so she would not get very far running in the woods. They were trotting fast, and she didn't want to fall from Sandy's back trussed up like this. She lay still, saving her energy for when she met her cousin.

Eventually, the pony slowed to a walk. They went downhill. She heard hooves splashing in water, and the roar of a waterfall. The pony lurched up and over what sounded like some rocks, and freezing spray drenched her feet. Then things went dark on the other side of the sack.

The horses' hooves echoed, so she knew

they had gone underground. There was a strong smell, noticeable even through the filthy sack. A chill went through her – dragon stink.

Finally the horses stopped, their snorts loud in the cave. The bloodbeards, who had grumbled and cursed most of the journey, went quiet.

"What took you so long?" a voice called.

Rhianna tensed as she recognised her cousin's sly tone.

"Had a bit of trouble," said the captain. "Her horse kept disappearing in the mist."

"Avalonian tricks," Mordred hissed. "Where's the animal now?"

"I don't know, Master," said the bloodbeard. "It ran off. You told me to grab the girl, not the horse. We got the Pendragon shield too."

"So I see. I'm glad you managed at least one

of the tasks I sent you to do." He paused at her feet, and Rhianna's skin prickled. "I hope you haven't damaged her? She's remarkably quiet."

Rhianna's breath came faster. She heard the tap of a crutch as her cousin limped nearer.

When she judged he was close enough, she jerked out her legs. She was rewarded by a grunt of pain. The bloodbeard captain chuckled.

"What are you laughing at?" Mordred yelled. "You almost ruined the whole operation, bringing Camelot's knights with you to Dragonland! What were you thinking of? If I hadn't sent those dragons to ambush them, you'd still be snivelling in their clutches now. All right, get the girl down off that pony and take her inside. The men know where to put her. I've got something to take care of out here. Then, my brave cousin…" He limped round to the other side of the pony and touched her cheek through the sack, making her shudder. "You and I are going to have a nice little chat, and you are going to tell me what you've done with that jewel your father took out of the Crown of Dreams."

"I'm not telling you anything!" Rhianna shouted through the sack, and he laughed.

"I see you know what I'm talking about. Good, that's a start." He limped away before she could swing her legs around to kick him again.

‡

The bloodbeards handled her with extra care after that, as if they were being watched. Two of them carried her through an echoing space to somewhere more muffled, where they set her down on something soft. Then they loosened the rope about her ankles.

Rhianna tensed, listening for clues. Where had her cousin got to? How many men were guarding her? She thought only two, but there might more out in the cave. She'd have to be ready to run fast.

As she gathered her courage, she heard the clank of a chain and felt something cold click shut around her ankle. She kicked frantically, but too late. They loosened the ropes about her sack and quickly stepped back.

By the time she'd fought her way out of the filthy thing, the bloodbeards had retreated down the tunnel, leaving her chained in a small alcove. Rhianna tugged at the chain, but it had been hammered into the rock and held firm. She flung the ropes after them with a furious shout. "Take this thing off me!" she yelled. "I'm King Arthur's daughter! You can't treat me like this! You'll be sorry…"

She tried to see where they had gone, but from her position she couldn't even see the waterfall that hid the entrance to the cave, though she could still hear its roar. With such a loud noise, nobody outside would hear her scream.

She hugged her knees, fighting tears. She wouldn't give Mordred the satisfaction of seeing her cry. She took a deep breath and looked around for something to use as a weapon. Her alcove was lit by a single candle, but it had been placed out of her reach. Bones were piled in the corners. She sat on a red cloak with a bloodstain on one corner. She touched the blood and turned cold.

A chuckle made her tense. "Not so tough

without your magic sword, are you, cousin?"

Her skin prickled as Mordred's crippled body filled the entrance to her prison. He leaned on a spear, and something glittered about his head.

"You haven't got Excalibur, either," Rhianna pointed out, trying to decide if the chain was long enough for her to kick him again. But he stayed out of reach in the shadows of the tunnel.

Mordred smiled. "Ah, but one of my dragons has. Don't worry, it'll keep the Sword of Light safe for me until I'm ready to ride to Camelot and claim my throne."

"They're not your dragons," she said, gritting her teeth. "And it's not your throne. It's King Arthur's, and when he returns from Avalon he's not going to be very pleased when he hears how you chained me up like a slave."

Mordred sighed. "We've already had this conversation. Your dear father is not going to return to the world of men for a very long time, if at all. Only the Grail of Stars has the power to command an unwilling soul back into its body before it is ready, and you'll never find the Grail without the knowledge stored in the Crown of Dreams. You didn't even take him the Sword of Light when you had the chance last year. You wanted to keep it for yourself, and look what happened… still, what can you expect when you give damsel a sword? Anyway, you're wrong, cousin. They *are* my dragons."

He limped forward into the candlelight, tossed back his cloak and smiled at her. He had washed and curled his hair so it hung across his scar, making him look quite handsome. He wore a black gauntlet over his stump, and silver and black tunic embroidered with his double-headed eagle. On his head sat a glittering crown with a green jewel glowing at his forehead – the same crown she had seen in her dream, and in Merlin's song pictures back in Avalon at the start of her quest.

He smiled triumphantly at her. "Suits me, doesn't it, cousin? This is the crown of the ancient Dragonlords, passed down through the Pendragon bloodline to the true heir. Whoever wears this crown can control dragons and command the forces of Annwn. So you see, the Sword of Light will soon be mine as well as your father's throne. An army of dragons and ghosts should take care of Camelot's walls, I think."

Rhianna's heart sank. All the strength ran

out of her. That bloodbeard had been telling the truth, after all.

"The Crown of Dreams," she whispered.

8

Dragon Riding

Dragon riders of great renown
Were those who wore the Pendragon crown.
The Jewel of Annwn shines far and wide
Yet its smallest stones do secrets hide.

At first, Rhianna felt like bursting into tears. Mordred leaned on his spear, watching her with his dark smile. The crown glittered on his head as if it had been made for him. Did it really give him control over dragons? If so, she'd as good as handed him Excalibur.

Then she saw the tense look in his eye and remembered the bloodbeards who had captured her saying: *Prince Mordred's obviously not as in control of them as he thinks he is.* A flicker of hope returned.

"But the Crown doesn't work for you, does it?" she said sweetly. "Not without King Arthur's jewel. That's why you haven't killed me – you need all the jewels before you can use its magic."

"It works well enough," he said through gritted teeth. He took a step closer, his fist tight on the spear.

She pressed back against the rock, acting scared. He might wear her father's crown, but he was still a cripple. If he came just a step or two closer, she might be able to kick that spear out from under him and turn it against him. Then she would make the bloodbeards let her go.

But Mordred stayed just out of reach of her chain. He laughed at her frustrated expression.

"Give it up, cousin. You're no shrinking damsel – I know your tricks. You're right, though, in a way. I need that jewel so I can destroy it and everything Arthur stood for before I can claim the Pendragon throne. I was informed you wore the stone around your neck, but it seems not. Tell me where it is, and maybe I'll let you live to see me crowned King of Camelot."

"Never!" Rhianna said.

Destroy her father's jewel? All his secrets would be lost.

He nodded, as if he'd expected her to say

as much. "Then it seems I'm going to have to persuade you to help me another way. If you're not worried about your own life, maybe you'll be slightly more worried about your little friends out there in the hills. They're all alone, you know, looking for you. I'm guessing, since you don't have it, that one of them has the jewel. Rather than waste any more time, I'll simply send my shadrake after them. The creature might have to kill your friends to get hold of the stone, but that'll save me the bother. So if they don't have it, now's the time to say."

He waited, a little smile playing on his lips.

She turned cold at the thought of the shadrake hunting Elphin and Cai. But if her cousin couldn't control ordinary dragons properly, how would he control the shadrake from Annwn?

"The shadrake can't hurt them," she said, hoping this was true. "Cai carries the Lance of Truth, and Elphin's got his harp."

"Ah yes. The second Light made by the hands of men, and the magic of Avalon… one useless in a squire's hands, the other useless against a creature of Annwn. Well, cousin, you'll find my power is stronger than you think. Watch and learn."

He closed his eyes, and the green jewel at the front of the crown began to glow. The air in the cave turned colder. "Come, shadrake!" Mordred called. "I wear the crown of the ancient Dragonlords who once rode you through the skies. I command you to return to the lair where you were born!"

At first nothing happened. Rhianna breathed again. He must be bluffing, trying to scare her. She quietly unbuckled Excalibur's empty scabbard. While he was distracted, maybe she could use it to hook the spear towards her?

But even as she coiled the belt ready to swing, a green flash lit up the tunnel behind Mordred, dazzling her. A dull boom echoed deep within the hillside, followed by scrabbling claws out in the cave. Frightened neighs came from the horses.

"I COME, PENDRAGON!" bellowed a familiar dragon voice.

An icy wind rushed up the tunnel, blowing out some of the candles. Small stones fell from the roof and a trickle of dust landed in her hair. Rhianna brushed it off, sweating a little. What if the stupid creature brought the whole hillside down on them?

"Not in here!" Mordred looked round in alarm. "Get after the Avalonian prince and that useless squire who carries the Lance of Truth, and kill them for me. Bring me any jewels you find on them. And while you're at it, bring me the Lance as well."

"WILL YOU RIDE WITH ME, PENDRAGON?"

Mordred's face twisted in sudden pain, and Rhianna saw her chance. She spun the scabbard across the floor, aiming for the spear he'd been using as a crutch.

The buckle end of her belt whipped around its shaft, jerking the dark knight off balance. He fell to his knees, and the green glow from the jewel faded. The Crown of Dreams slipped off his head and rolled across the floor.

Rhianna dived after it at the same time as

Mordred. The chain tugged at her ankle, but not before her fingers closed about the crown. It was unexpectedly hot, and she almost let go again. Mordred grabbed it too, having abandoned his spear when he realised the trick.

They were evenly matched. His crippled leg handicapped him, just like her chained ankle. But he only had one hand, and he needed that to grip the crown. She reached for his spear with her free hand and brought it down as hard as she could across his knuckles. He let go with a yell of rage and called for his men to help him.

Fending off the dark knight with the spear, Rhianna retreated against the wall and did the only thing she could think of. She took a deep breath and jammed the Crown of Dreams on to her own head.

❀

Her heart pounded with a mixture of excitement and terror. She had no idea what to expect. Would its magic work for her, or would it kill her?

At first the crown felt too big, and she thought it would slip over her eyes and make her look stupid. Then it tightened, and she felt little spots of heat from the jewels, warmest on her forehead where the green stone still glowed faintly. There was a cold patch near the back – was it where her father's missing jewel belonged?

A great hush surrounded her. Then the whispers started inside her head.

"*Who is she?*"

"*A damsel…*"

"*Another witch like Le Fay?*"

"No, a warrior maid of the blood... but a girl cannot inherit the throne."

"Best get rid of her so the crown can pass to the prince..."

She almost snatched the thing off again. But she knew she wouldn't get another chance to help her friends. She closed her eyes like Mordred had done and thought of the dragon.

"Shadrake!" she called. "Shadrake, can you hear me? I wear the Crown of Dreams now. I'll ride with you. *I'm* not afraid."

Dark wings flapped inside her head, banishing the whispers. Something pressed between her eyes. She felt the dragon's surprise... then suddenly the pressure eased, and her spirit was flying above the clouds through a red and gold sunset.

It was so beautiful, she forgot her body was chained in the dragon's lair at the mercy of her cousin and his bloodbeards. It felt like a dream, only better, because she could feel the wind on her cheeks and smell the ice in the air. She was spirit-riding the shadrake, just as Merlin had done before he found his falcon body!

Through rags of mist far below, she saw a wooded valley and a river with two white horses standing on the bank. A small figure dressed in Avalonian green knelt beside the water, studying some prints in the mud. His back was turned to the dragon as it shrieked in recognition and dived, carrying Rhianna's spirit helplessly towards him.

"Elphin!" she yelled, forgetting he couldn't possibly hear her. "Elphin, look behind you!"

Her viewpoint swerved back towards the

wood as a grey horse came galloping out of the trees, ridden by a plump squire clinging to a lance. The dragon's eye focused on the glittering weapon, and she felt its desire for the shiny thing. The boy pointed the lance determinedly at her and shouted a challenge.

"Cai!" she gasped. "Don't! It's me—"

The shadrake back-winged in confusion. She saw Elphin spring to his feet and run for his harp, which he'd left tied to Evenstar's saddle. The shadrake breathed a long plume of ice, freezing the surface of the river. Evenstar misted one way to avoid it, and Alba – the second horse – misted the other.

Glad to see her mare had escaped the bloodbeards, and forgetting she was in the body of a dragon, she chased the little horse. Alba fled over the river, cracking the ice and misting again. The shadrake shook its head in annoyance.

Elphin went down on one knee, looking very small and alone. His harp shimmered in the sunset, and his thin face was raised towards her. She heard a faint ripple of Avalonian music. For a heartbeat his violet eyes met hers, and she heard his voice singing in her head.

"Four Lights stand against the dark... The Sword Excalibur that was forged in Avalon..."

"Leave my friends alone!" she commanded the shadrake, suddenly seeing how to distract it. "You don't have to take their treasure. I know where there's a beautiful, shiny sword!" She summoned a memory of the red dragon carrying off Excalibur, and the shadrake shrieked again and abandoned its attack.

With strong wing beats, they flew over

the wood and up into the mountains. She looked down and saw the old stone circle where she'd been captured flash beneath them. The shadrake crossed the road where the dragons had ambushed their party, but she could see no sign of the knights. A chill went through her. Where had they got to? She hoped they weren't dead.

Then she saw a rock shaped like a finger on a mountain top, and glimpsed the entrance to a cave. Smoke curled out of the hillside. As the shadrake flapped closer, her heart beat faster and she knew it had brought her to the right place. The red dragon that had taken her sword launched itself out of the cave, screaming a challenge and belching out flame. The shadrake breathed ice in answer, and the two dragons met in a shower of icy rain.

"No," she gasped. "No, don't fight—"

Laughter broke the spell, and something snapped in Rhianna's head as her spirit whirled back to the shadrake's lair.

She opened her eyes, expecting to see Mordred and his bloodbeards. But Morgan Le Fay's ghost sat on a pile of blackened bones, blocking the way into the alcove and stopping Rhianna's spirit from returning to her body. The witch's ghost looked more solid than she had at the North Wall in the spring. Her hair glimmered with green light.

"So, Rhianna Pendragon," she said with another laugh. "You managed to get the Crown of Dreams off my idiot of a son and spirit-ride the shadrake. Enjoying the experience, were you?"

Rhianna scowled at the ghost in frustration.

"Go away. I'm not scared of you. You're dead. You can't hurt me."

The witch chuckled. "Clearly you've no idea what wearing that crown really means. This is one of the gates to Annwn, where the dead can pass into the world of the living. You heard them when you put the crown on, didn't you? The voices of the old Pendragon lords? So tell me what I want to know, and maybe I'll let your spirit return to your body. I believe my son asked what you did with your father's jewel. You haven't brought it with you, so where did you leave it?"

"Think I'm going to tell *you*?" Rhianna said, trying to slip past the ghost.

"Yes, I think you are," said the witch. "Because I wore that Crown too, you know, and I've had more practice in using it than you have."

Rhianna felt dizzy. To her alarm, a vision of Arianrhod sitting in Camelot's dungeon flashed unbidden through her head.

Her friend's eyes widened. "Lady Rhia!" she said, springing to her feet and staring about her in confusion. "What are *you* doing here? Are you a dream...?"

"Oh, how very clever of you!" Morgan Le Fay smiled at Arianrhod and clapped her ghostly hands. "The missing jewel's still at Camelot, isn't it? In the one place nobody will think to look, locked in the dungeon with my poor little ex-maid – who is accused of witchcraft when, for the first time in her miserable life, she's actually free of me. How delicious! I think Mordred's going to enjoy this."

"Except I smashed your mirror so you can't tell him, can you?" Rhianna said.

But the witch was still laughing. She waved her hand through Arianrhod's shadow, making it fade away. "You're forgetting the Crown of Dreams, my dear. It records the secrets of every Pendragon who wears it, including yours."

"No…" she whispered, realising the mistake she'd made in putting on the crown before she fully understood the magic.

Morgan Le Fay chuckled. "Oh yes, as soon as my son wears the Crown again he'll see where you left your pathetic jewel. And that's not all. Merlin probably forgot to tell you, but that pretty green jewel at the front contains the secrets of the first Dragonlords, back in the days when Pendragons were not concerned with boring things such as Round Tables and knightly codes. They rode dragons, flying with the storm, taking what they wanted, when they wanted it."

The witch's eyes flashed.

"Then the Romans came with their roads and their hot baths, and Arthur built Camelot in their image. My brother preferred dragons carved into his throne and woven on his tapestries rather than living in his hills. So he sent his knights to kill them. But they didn't find them all, and there are still some breeding pairs in Dragonland. When my son takes the throne, we'll get rid of Arthur's silly dreams of chivalry and restore the old ways."

Rhianna was starting to feel panicky. If she didn't get back into her body soon, Mordred might do something horrible to it. "But Mordred can't take the throne until he's destroyed my father's jewel, can he? That's why he wants it so badly – while it's still safe, he can't destroy King Arthur's dreams for Camelot."

"Oh, aren't you the clever one," said Morgan Le Fay. "I almost wish you'd been my daughter. Maybe we should make you into Mordred's queen. He'll need someone to bear his heirs when he takes Camelot's throne."

"I'd rather die!" Rhianna said, reaching with her spirit for the green jewel that held the secret of dragon riding. Could she persuade the shadrake to help her escape? The witch's ghost wavered as a wing flapped inside her head.

Morgan Le Fay pursed her lips. "Still fighting, my dear? What a stubborn damsel you are. On second thoughts, I don't think my son will be able to handle you. You're rather more of a threat than we anticipated. So now we're sure you haven't brought the stone with you, I think it's best if we just bury you in here. It's a pity you have to die, but you give people hope, and hope is a dangerous thing. I'd love to talk longer, but I have to go and help my son open the Gate now. Have a good death, Rhianna Pendragon. I'll see you on the other side very soon."

※

The witch disappeared as someone snatched the crown from Rhianna's head. She jolted back into her body to find the rock shaking around her and showers of stones rattling down from the tunnel roof.

Mordred scowled down at her, holding the crown and breathing heavily. She must have dropped the spear. His bloodbeard captain held the point to her throat. More bloodbeards crowded into the alcove, staring nervously at the cracks appearing in the roof.

Mordred waved them back. "Get out of here, you fools! Wait for me outside. I'll take care of this."

He shook his head at her. "That was stupid, cousin! What did you think you were trying to do? I've spent weeks learning how to use this crown! It killed my mother, you know. It's dangerous if you don't know what you're doing, and now you seem to have brought the entire mountain down on our heads."

"That wasn't me – it was your crazy mother. She's going to open the Gate of Annwn! You've got to stop her."

"Really? And why would I want to do that?" He glanced up in alarm as more grit fell from the roof into his hair. "I'm afraid I can't stay to

chat any longer. I'd run if I were you, cousin…
oh, but I forgot, someone seems to have chained
you to the rock. Suppose you think I'm going
to release you so you can escape? You should
have tried that trick before we found out you
don't have your father's jewel."

"You can't destroy it!" she said desperately.
"You don't know what secrets it might contain."

He paused, and she thought he might
unchain her. Then another shower of stones
fell between them, and he smiled. "Good try,
cousin. But you don't know either, and I don't
need you to discover them now I've got the
Crown. I doubt my uncle's secrets are of much
interest, anyway." He limped back down the
tunnel gripping his bloodbeard's shoulder.

Rhianna blinked after him through the
clouds of dust. She heard the horses leave

the cave, then a loud rumble deep inside the mountain. A chill went down her spine as she remembered the witch's words. *We'll just bury you in here.* She tugged at the chain in terror and opened her mouth to call him back.

The tunnel roof collapsed in a rush of rock and billowing clouds of foul-smelling dust. Ghostly warriors howled out of the depths of the mountain and poured past her in a glowing green river. She huddled against the rock, pulled the bloodstained cloak over her head and made herself as small as possible to avoid the falling stones.

"When I get out of here, you'll be sorry!" she yelled.

The air that had come up the tunnel suddenly cut off as the alcove crumbled around her, and her world went dark.

DARK ARMY

Mordred clung to his horse's neck as it galloped through the waterfall after his fleeing men. Boulders splashed down around him, and the river roared and foamed underfoot. They were halfway down the valley before he dared pull up. He looked back at the pile of rocks that blocked the cave mouth and shook his head in exasperation.

"It's your own fault, cousin," he muttered. "I gave you a chance! Why couldn't you bring the stupid jewel with you, like a normal damsel would have done?"

"That was close, Master," said his

bloodbeard captain, drawing rein beside him. He frowned at the cave, too. "Do you want us to dig her out?"

Mordred pulled himself together. "No! She's done us a favour, burying herself in there. We should be able to get into Camelot while the knights and her friends are still looking for her here in Dragonland."

"She might not be dead," the bloodbeard pointed out.

"If she isn't, then she'll soon wish she was," Mordred growled. "I'll be sitting on Arthur's throne by the time she digs her way out of there with her bare hands. Now stand back – my mother promised me an army."

He jammed the Crown of Dreams on his head. The bloodbeards drew back warily as the green jewel began to glow.

A wind howled along the valley, whipping up the river. Then a ghostly green horse leaped out of the hill through the curtain of water, ridden by a warrior wearing a winged helm and wielding a large axe. Behind him poured a stream of other ghostly horses and riders. The waterfall glimmered green as they passed through it and entered the world of men. All were armed, and all had fierce expressions with death in their eyes.

The bloodbeards' horses plunged and snorted. The pony the captain had used to bring the girl here broke free and galloped off, plunging into the flood up to its belly. The captain turned his horse to give chase.

"Let the stupid animal go," Mordred snapped. "It can drown for all I care."

His stallion laid back its ears as the warrior

in the winged helm rode closer. He gripped his reins tightly for courage and faced the ghost.

"So the new Pendragon calls us out of Annwn to fight again," growled the warrior, casting a glance at the bloodbeards and their trembling horses. "Not much of an army. I expected more from a grandson of mine."

"King Uther!" whispered one of the older bloodbeards. "It's Uther Pendragon, back from the dead!"

The other men muttered uneasily and drew closer together.

"My Saxon allies will be waiting for us at Camelot," Mordred said, more confidently than he felt. "My cousin made a treaty with them last year, but they'll soon change sides again when they see the way things are going.

We've got boats waiting to take us across the
Summer Sea. I assume your – er, men – can
ride across water?"

He tried to count the ghostly warriors.
But they kept fading and then reappearing
again in the green light cast by the jewel,
making him feel queasy. The Crown burned
his forehead. It didn't fit as well as it had
before his cousin wore it – curse the girl,
who'd have thought she would dare snatch
it off him and try to use it herself?

"Water is no barrier to spirits," said Uther
with a harsh laugh. "Let's get going! I'm keen
to see this great castle my son is supposed
to have built after my death. Oh, and your
mother sent this for you."

Mordred had been about to remove the
crown before he made a fool of himself.

He barely caught the black gauntlet the ghost threw at him. Cold shivered through him – *a thing of Annwn!* Then the stump of his right arm began to itch, and he realised the gauntlet still contained a human hand – his own right hand, which Arthur had chopped off with Excalibur at the battle of Camlann, and the shadrake had carried into Annwn when Rhianna banished it last year.

His captain's expression grew fearful. The man had reason to be wary of it, since he'd helped Mordred use its dark magic to torture prisoners during the hunt for Excalibur. Mordred tucked the severed fist into his belt with a smile.

Uther's gaze followed it. "Morgan said you used to be a pretty boy," he said with another chuckle. "Shame Arthur cut you up so badly in the battle. But when you join us in Annwn, your wounds will not matter. You'll be able to ride with us, whole and strong again, without pain."

Mordred scowled at his grandfather. "I'm not going to join you in Annwn, old man," he snapped. "When Camelot's throne is mine and I've learned all the secrets of this Crown, I'm going to send out every man who can ride a horse to look for the Grail of Stars. I'll make myself whole that way."

"Did you hear that? My grandson thinks he's going to escape death." Uther's ghost laughed. All the other ghosts laughed too, rippling green across the river.

Mordred shuddered. It was getting dark in the valley, and Annwn's chill had worked its way into his bones. He could hear his mother trying to tell him something, but it would have to wait until his head stopped hurting. He snatched off the crown and hung it from his belt beside his dark fist. To his relief, as the green glow died, the ghosts faded to vague glimmers in the night.

"We're wasting time," he yelled at his bloodbeards. "To Camelot! My throne awaits."

9

Gate of Annwn

Darkness was Rhianna's fate
Buried at Annwn's ancient gate,
Where ghosts and shadows haunt the hills
And river of death from the rockface spills.

R hianna opened her eyes to darkness and
silence. She felt bruised all over. She
uncurled, threw off the cloak in a shower of
small stones and shook the dust from her hair.
She could see nothing at all. Was she dead?

She crawled warily towards where she remembered her cousin standing, and something behind her clanked... the stupid chain. She felt around in the dark until she found the sword belt she'd thrown at Mordred and spent some time trying to open the manacle with the point of the buckle. But she couldn't see what she was doing and kept stabbing her fingers in the dark. She wished she had listened to Arianrhod and put some pins in her hair. She might have picked the lock with them.

Tears came when she thought of how the witch had tricked her into putting her friend in danger. Then she thought of her cousin's smile as he'd limped away down the tunnel and tightened her fist on her empty scabbard.

He'd left her in here to die!

"You won't take the throne," she said

through gritted teeth. "It's my father's, and I'm going to get out of here and stop you."

"*That's my brave girl,*" said a voice.

Rhianna's stomach jumped. She spun round, clutching the buckle like a weapon, and stared into the dark. Had one of Mordred's bloodbeards got trapped down here with her? But it didn't sound like something a bloodbeard would say.

Then her Avalonian armour began to glimmer, showing her King Arthur's ghost looking very pale and thin against a slab of rock. It seemed the roof had collapsed, by some miracle missing her on the way down and creating a pocket of air.

"Father!" she gasped. "What are you doing here? This is the Gate to Annwn! You mustn't go there, or I'll never get your soul back into your body in Avalon… how did you get in?"

"*Rock is no barrier to a spirit,*" the ghost said with a smile. "*The magic of the Crown shines brightly. You were not hard to find, daughter. But you must get out of here before the rest of the roof falls.*"

"What do you think I'm trying to do?" she muttered, eyeing the cracks in the rock above her head.

"*Try the other end.*" The ghost pointed to the place where her chain had been staked to the wall, and she realised a crack ran right through the fastening.

Her heart leaped in hope. She groped her way back along the chain and poked the buckle into the crack. After a bit of work and a broken nail, the stake dropped into her lap.

She gathered up the hateful chain in relief,

wrapped it around her waist and fastened her sword belt over the top to keep it out of the way. Grinning, she sprang to her feet and hit her head on the roof. "Ow!" she muttered, seeing stars.

"*Keep your head low,*" her father's ghost advised. "*The tunnel is not blocked, but you'll need to move some stones.*"

Rhianna rubbed her head, dropped back to her knees and crawled over to the tunnel. She heaved a large stone out of the way and scraped at the rubble, enlarging the hole. It still looked very small. She'd hoped to see daylight, but more darkness waited ahead. She thought of the underwater tunnel she'd swum through to find Nimue's cave and Excalibur. This was no worse, not really.

She took a deep breath and wormed her

way through the foul-smelling dark. She had to stop several times to move more rubble out of the way, squeezing the stones past her and pushing them back along the tunnel with her feet. By the time she tasted fresher air ahead, her fingers and toes were bruised and bleeding.

With a final rattle of stones, she crawled out of the tunnel into the larger cave the bloodbeards had carried her through. Then, she'd had a sack over her head. Now, the glimmer of her armour showed her piles of treasure and pale bones.

She stood up warily and picked her way across the lair. There were sharp things underfoot, and no sign of her boots. She found a rusty dagger among the dragon's treasure and used it to cut up an old cloak that had been lying near the bones. She tied the strips around her sore feet. Then she studied her prison.

A great wall of rubble blocked the entrance to the lair. Boulders the size of horses reached all the way up to the roof. Her heart sank. She'd never shift those on her own. Could she dig another tunnel between them? She carefully began to remove the smaller stones that filled the gaps between the larger rocks, using the dagger to lever them out.

Meanwhile, her father's ghost sat down on a pile of the dragon's treasure and stared at a heap of rags and charred bones lying at his feet. He frowned slightly, as if searching for a memory, then touched the body.

"*Sister*," he said sadly. "*Why did you have to oppose me?*"

A chill went through Rhianna as she recognised the blackened bones as those

Morgan Le Fay's spirit had been sitting on earlier.

She glanced uneasily at her father. He kept fading and then shimmering back into view with a start, like someone trying not to doze off. His ghost looked even paler and thinner than it had the first time she'd seen him. Was the witch's spirit trying to lure him through the Gate to Annwn?

"Tell me more about the Crown of Dreams," she said to distract him. "Merlin told me its jewels contain secrets, which can only be passed on to another Pendragon. You gave one of those jewels to my mother and told her to give it to me, didn't you? What secret does it contain?"

The ghost frowned at her. "*Something to do with the Grail, I think... things are hazy now my spirit's out of my body, but Mordred must not wear that crown with my jewel restored.*"

"No chance of that!" she said, snatching up a broken spear to use as a lever on the boulders. "He wants to destroy it, not restore it." She had to get out of here before her cousin got the jewel off Arianrhod.

Her father's ghost became even paler. "*Then we haven't got much time, daughter. If Mordred destroys my jewel and wears the Crown of Dreams at the Round Table, my knights will have no choice but to give him the throne of Camelot. The Crown chooses the rightful heir according to the old Pendragon bloodline, and if my jewel is missing there'll be no record of you. Mordred will be the only candidate.*"

Rhianna paused in her digging to stare at him.

"That's stupid! The knights won't give the throne to Mordred. They know I'm your daughter now – you were there at midsummer when the queen told everyone I was heir to the throne. Sir Bors and Sir Lancelot aren't going to let some silly magic crown decide who rules them! Don't they write important things like that down? They wrote down the treaty I made with the Saxons last year. Anyway, the throne's still yours! When you return from Avalon, you'll take the Crown back from Mordred, won't you?"

She tried not to think of what might happen if she failed her quest and couldn't bring her father back.

The king sighed. *"I can remember so little of Camelot. It's like a dream to me now. Maybe you are a dream, too? My daughter, who rides a fairy horse and wields Excalibur... it sounds like one of old Merlin's songs. And now Merlin's out of the way, it'll be easy enough for Mordred to wipe us both from history."* His ghost faded again.

"Merlin's not dead yet." At least, she hoped not. Where was the druid when they needed him? But even a small hawk wouldn't be able to get through this wall of rock.

"You can't rely on Merlin," her father said, frowning again as if trying to remember something else.

"Then I'd better hurry up and get out of here so I can remind everyone we exist, hadn't I?" she said, forcing a grin. She didn't like to see her father so sad. She hoped he would cheer up a bit once she got him back into his body.

Renewing her attack on the rubble, she jammed the spear under a boulder and leaned all her weight on it. The spear snapped, and she stumbled against the rocks, bruising her shoulder.

She flung the broken pieces of wood at the blockage in frustration. "Oh, this is hopeless! I'll never get out this way."

Suddenly, the air in the cave seemed less fresh. Rhianna sat down on the treasure to catch her breath and looked for her father's ghost, barely visible now in the shadows. What had he said?

Rocks are no barrier to a spirit.

"I know!" she said. "You can walk out through the rock the same way you got in here and find Elphin and Cai. They're in the woods two valleys away… or they were when I last saw them."

How long ago had she worn the crown and

seen her friends through the shadrake's eyes? She could have been lying buried under this mountain for days. Mordred might already have taken her father's jewel off Arianrhod and be sitting on the throne of Camelot. She shook her head, refusing to think of that.

"They saw you at Lady Nimue's lake when you chased Mordred and his men away in the summer," she continued. "So maybe they'll be able to see you again. Then you can lead them up here, and they'll bring the knights to dig me out."

It seemed so simple, she wondered why she hadn't thought of it before.

He gave her a worried look. *"I hate to leave you here in the dark with Morgan Le Fay, daughter. She is strong in this place. She might try to drag your spirit through the Gate."*

Rhianna forced another grin. "She already tried, but I've got to die first and she can't kill me herself. Mordred had some candles down here. I'll find them when you're gone, and keep working on this side until my friends and the knights get here."

Her father's ghost reached for her hands. She felt a brief warmth as his fingers passed through hers. "*You'll make a stronger Pendragon than Mordred,*" he said. "*I'm proud to have such a daughter.*"

Then he got up and walked into the rock, and the last glimmer of light from her armour died.

❈

Her father was proud of her. Even if she didn't get out of here, she'd die happy.

But she wasn't going to die. She wouldn't give Mordred and his witch mother the satisfaction.

She spent a bit of time searching for candles, but Mordred must either have taken them with him, or they had been buried under the rubble with the rest of her stuff. She didn't know how she would have lit them, anyway.

She worked more slowly in the dark, feeling around every stone before she removed it, in case she made a mistake and brought the rest of the mountain crashing down on her head. Sweat trickled down her back every time she heard an avalanche in the depths of the hill, but she didn't take off her Avalonian armour. Its magic had protected her so far.

Time passed. How much time, she had no way of telling, except by the ache in her arms and a terrible thirst caused by the dust in her throat. She wondered if Mordred had found out where she'd left her father's jewel yet. She kept thinking of her cousin marching through Camelot's corridors, and of Arianrhod's promise to guard the jewel with her life.

It was all taking too long. There had to be another way out.

She stopped to catch her breath and looked thoughtfully at Morgan Le Fay's body. Could she summon the witch's spirit, and trick her aunt into using her dark magic to make the rocks at the entrance collapse again? She shook her head. No, there was too much danger they would fall on her this time, and she no longer had the Crown or the mirror to do the summoning.

She clenched her fists. She hadn't come so far to die here alone in the dark. *Think, Rhianna, think.*

In the silence, she heard a faint dripping overhead. Of course – water! There had been a river outside the cave and a waterfall feeding it. Where had that water come from, if not out of the mountain?

With new hope, she worked her way back across the lair, stopping every few steps to listen carefully. When a drop of water landed on her cheek, her heart beat faster. She hitched up her chain and, carefully feeling for every hand and foothold, began to climb the rubble towards the sound.

"Don't fall," she muttered. "Just don't fall."

She climbed higher, glad that she couldn't see the void beneath her. After what seemed forever, she felt damp rock under her bare toes. Having no boots actually helped, and she laughed. That bloodbeard had done her a favour, taking them from her. But the rock here was more unstable. A whole handful came away, and she slid back down the rubble.

She pressed her face to the cliff, listening to the thud of her heart and the patter of stones falling into the depths of the mountain. The tinkling sounded louder now, coming from above – the music of Avalon. Hardly daring to believe, she looked up and saw a watery sunbeam shining though a small hole in the rock.

"Elphin…" she whispered.

She scrambled up the rest of the way and pressed her face to the hole. She sucked at the sweet, bright air and punched her fist through.

A great slab of rock went sliding away in a rush of green water.

She squinted into the sunlight. She had emerged at the top of the waterfall, which tumbled down into a flooded valley. Four tiny horses picked their way upriver towards the blocked entrance to the cave. Two of the horses trotted on the surface of the water, leaving trails of mist, the one in front ridden by a small figure with a shining harp. The third horse splashed and stumbled over the avalanched rocks behind them, carrying Cai with his lance. Sandy swam riderless behind.

Rhianna's heart lifted. She waved her arms. "Elphin! Cai! Up here!"

But the roar of the waterfall drowned her voice. She looked at the slippery rocks leading down beside it and shook her head. She'd done enough mountain climbing for one day.

She pinched her nose and made a leap through the water into the sunlight.

Wind whistled in her ears…. trees flashed past… water roared around her… and she entered the river with a splash. She barely had time to take a breath, and she'd forgotten the chain, which weighed her down. But the thought of Mordred on his way to Camelot with the Crown of Dreams kept her going. She kicked strongly for the surface and came up gasping for air. She managed to grab a rock before her armour and the chain could drag her back down again. Clinging on with one arm, she gulped handfuls of the cold, clear water and laughed.

"I'm still alive, cousin!" she yelled. "Do you hear me? I'm alive!"

⚜

Small hooves, glinting with Avalonian silver, trotted towards her over the water. A soft nose lowered and sniffed at her. *You are very wet*, observed her mist horse. *Evenstar's rider is worried. He thinks you are buried inside the dragon's hill.*

Rhianna wiped hair out of her eyes and blinked up at the cliff she'd jumped from. It was higher than she'd thought. Down here, she could barely hear Elphin's music over the noise of the water.

She laughed again. "Help me out, my beautiful one," she said.

The mare obligingly let Rhianna catch hold of her tail, trotted to the bank and pulled her out of the river. Rhianna lay in the mud, too exhausted to move, staring up at the sky. She felt like going to sleep. Then Alba whinnied, and the music stopped. Elphin's six-fingered hand pushed the mare's muzzle out of the way. His anxious face stared down at her.

"Rhia?" he whispered, his eyes the deepest purple she'd ever seen them. "Where does it hurt?"

"All over," she groaned, which was true. Now that she was out of the dragon's lair, every muscle ached and her cuts and bruises had begun to throb.

Elphin touched a bruise on her cheek with gentle fingers. His purple gaze took in the chain still locked about her ankle. "Don't move, Rhia. You might have broken something. I'll play my harp for you."

Cai's flushed face appeared on her other side.

"Damsel Rhianna!" he gasped. "What did Mordred do to you? We were really worried when we found Alba. We've been tracking you for days! Elphin's good at it, but there was some magic at work around those stones. Then the river flooded, and those sneaky bloodbeards hid their trail in the water. We only knew this was the right valley when we found poor Sandy trying to swim down it. Elphin used his magic to find the path around the waterfall, but when we saw the avalanche behind it we thought the worst... how did you escape?"

"Cai," she said, coughing up water. "Now you're making my ears hurt! I heard your music coming through the water and climbed out, of course... you didn't see my father's ghost then? I sent him to find you."

The boy shook his head.

Rhianna sighed. Obviously, the magic of the Lance alone wasn't strong enough to make the king's ghost visible to her friends.

"Never mind, I expect he's around somewhere. You found me, and that's the main thing… don't fuss, Elphin." She pushed her friend's harp away. "I'm all right. The last thing I want is to fall asleep now. *How* long did you say you'd been tracking me?"

"Three days," Cai said. "And a night."

Rhianna struggled to her feet. Were three days enough for Mordred to get to Camelot with an army and break through the gates? It had taken them and the knights three days to ride here the long way.

"We've got to hurry!" She swayed on her feet, but clutched Alba's mane before Elphin could make her lie back down again. "Where are Sir Lancelot and the others?"

"Dunno." Cai bit his lip and glanced at Elphin. "Still looking for us, I expect. Elphin wouldn't wait for them. He said they'd slow us down, and we had to find you before Mordred killed you."

Rhianna looked back at the collapsed cave and shuddered. "He left me in there to die," she said. "But it takes more than a few rocks to kill me."

She tried to vault into Alba's saddle and tripped over the chain. Elphin pressed his lips together, closed one hand around the manacle and played a ripple on his harp with the other. Sweat sprang out on his brow. The metal sparkled and melted from her foot.

Rhianna stared at the shining puddle in the grass and let him help her up on her mare.

"Your magic's getting stronger," she said. "You couldn't do that for my mother's chain in the summer."

"He'll do any kind of magic for you," Cai muttered. "Where are your boots?"

"Buried in the shadrake's lair somewhere, I expect – I'm not going back for them now." She turned Alba impatiently. "We have to find Excalibur and the knights and get back to Camelot as soon as we can. Mordred's got the Crown of Dreams. If we don't stop him, he's going to destroy my father's jewel and all its secrets, and use the crown to wipe King Arthur's name from history!"

10

Dragons

A finger of rock did point the way
To mountain high at close of day,
Where deep inside the dragon's hoard
Harp and Lance shall find the Sword.

Since none of them knew which way the knights had gone, they decided to look for Excalibur first. If they returned to the place where the shadrake had attacked her friends, Rhianna thought she would remember the way to the red dragon's lair from there. She wasn't sure what they would do if they found the shadrake waiting for them, but she'd think of something.

Elphin and Cai wanted to know everything, of course. What Mordred had said to her, and exactly how she'd escaped. As they trotted back downriver, Rhianna told them most of it. She didn't tell them how scared she'd been when the roof collapsed, or what her father's ghost had said about his jewel containing something about the Grail. She wanted to ask Merlin about that, if the silly bird ever turned up again.

"So the Crown killed Morgan Le Fay?" Elphin said thoughtfully. "I wonder why?"

"Because she's an evil witch, of course," Cai said. "I hope it kills Mordred as well! Chaining Damsel Rhianna in the dark like that and leaving her to die… just wait till I see the traitor again! I'll knock him off his horse and chain *him* in the dark, see how he likes it." He swung his lance around to demonstrate, and Rhianna ducked.

"Careful," she said, laughing as her armour glittered in response. "Or Mordred will be out of a job."

Cai flushed. "Sorry."

"Your armour must have saved your life in that cave," Elphin said. "A good thing those bloodbeards didn't take that off you as well as your shield and your boots. Maybe Father's smith put more magic into it than we thought."

"A good thing she wasn't carrying Excalibur, you mean," Cai said. "Or Mordred would have the Sword of Light now, never mind the Crown."

"If I'd had Excalibur, his men would never have captured me in the first place, you dolt!" Rhianna said with a smile. She frowned at a track that led away from the river up into the hills. "This way."

"Are you sure?" Cai said.

"Of course I'm sure. I've been this way before."

When she closed her eyes, she could see the cave with its rocky finger as clearly as when she'd worn the Crown of Dreams and spirit-ridden the shadrake. The only trouble was, everything looked different from the ground. Trees and hills kept getting in the way.

"What if the dragon doesn't want to give Excalibur back when we get there?"

"Then you'll have to prove you can use that lance you carry, won't you?" she said, wishing the boy would shut up for once and let her concentrate.

Cai went quiet.

They rode in silence for a while. Around them, the woods steamed in the sun, reminding Rhianna of the dragons flaming the knights. She felt a bit guilty when she thought of how worried they must be about her. But once she got Excalibur back, she might be able to use its magic to let them know she was all right.

Recognising another landmark, she urged Alba into a canter. Cai kept up well enough on the big grey, and even Sandy didn't get left too far behind without a rider to carry. But it was obviously going to take them longer to reach the dragon's lair than it had taken the shadrake to fly there. The sun was going down behind the hills by the time they reached the old stone circle where the bloodbeards had captured her.

She slowed Alba, her neck prickling in memory. She had a sense of being watched… then something small and feathered zipped past her ear.

Rhianna's hand flew to her empty scabbard. Remembering she didn't have Excalibur, she drew her rusty dagger and stared at the shadows between the stones looking for an enemy. But this time it was not a bloodbeard arrow. Instead, a small, blue-grey falcon landed on the end of Cai's lance.

"It's Merlin!" Cai said, nearly dropping the lance as his horse danced sideways.

Alba shook her silver mane. *He nearly made me mist*, the mare snorted.

Rhianna scowled at the bedraggled little bird in a mixture of relief and annoyance.

"Merlin! Where have you *been*?"

The merlin opened its beak and screeched at her.

She shook her head, amused. "It's no good scolding me – I can't hear a word you're saying. You'll have to wait until I've got Excalibur back."

The merlin kept on scolding. Cai blinked at it in surprise. "He says you're a very foolish girl, and you're lucky your soul's not trapped in Annwn with Morgan Le Fay's by now," he reported. "Spirit-riding a dragon is dangerous enough, let alone a shadrake!"

Elphin nodded. "He's right about that, Rhia."

The shining spear lets the bird talk to the human boy, Alba informed her.

She made a face, feeling a bit left out.

"Just because *he* couldn't manage it…" she muttered, remembering how the druid had tried to borrow the shadrake's body after Morgan Le Fay had ambushed them when they first came over from Avalon.

The merlin screeched again, and Cai's eyes went wide. "Oh Damsel Rhianna, this is bad! He says Mordred's used the Crown to call an army of ghosts out of Annwn and is crossing the Summer Sea. Opening the dark Gate caused a flood, so he can take his boats right across the marshes. They'll be at Camelot by tonight."

A chill went through Rhianna. "Let me talk to him," she said. She held out her wrist for the merlin, but it refused to leave Cai's lance, which glittered faintly in the last of the sun.

"Mordred must be taking a short cut,"

Elphin's eyes whirled violet. "We might be able to catch him on our mist horses. But if the roads are flooded, the knights will have to go the long way round – their horses can't gallop over water like Alba and Evenstar can." He listened to the druid again. "Merlin says the knights headed back to the border so they wouldn't get trapped in Dragonland by the floods. We should go and meet them, Rhia."

She looked back the way they had come and gathered up Alba's reins. "No. I can't fight Mordred without Excalibur."

"But what if *we* get trapped in Dragonland?" Cai wailed.

"Alba and Evenstar won't get trapped," she said impatiently. "You'll just have to wait here with Sandy until the roads are open again."

Cai paled.

"I've got a better idea," Elphin said, fingering the spiral pathfinder around his neck. "Merlin, does this stone circle work like the one at Camelot?"

The bird cocked its head and eyed the stones. It fluffed up its feathers and chattered something. Cai looked a bit relieved.

Elphin nodded. "He says it's very old and some of the stones are broken, but it still has power. Between us, we might be able to use it to open the spiral path and transport the knights through to Camelot's circle before Mordred gets there."

"Then what are we waiting for?" Rhianna said. "Someone go and fetch the knights, while I get my sword back from that dragon."

Of course Elphin and Cai refused to let her face the dragons alone, and started an argument over who should stay to protect her. In the end, they decided to send Merlin back to the knights with the message. Cai wrote it on a piece of bark, with much advice from the merlin and face-pulling, while Rhianna fiddled with Alba's mane and stared impatiently at the hills.

"You don't have to write a song," she said. "Just tell them to follow my merlin to the stone circle and meet us there. At this rate, Mordred will be sitting on the throne of Camelot before you're finished."

"Writing's more difficult than you think, Damsel Rhianna," Cai said with a frown. "I can't remember how to spell all the words."

"Does that matter?" She glanced at Elphin.

"Don't look at me, Rhia," her friend said.

"Writing's a human thing. In Avalon we just have our songs, and they're hard enough to learn."

Rhianna sighed. She must ask Arianrhod to teach her how to read and write when they got back to Camelot. If Arianrhod was still alive after Mordred had finished with her.

She clenched her fist on her empty scabbard and tried to be patient with the squire.

Eventually, after more finger-pecking and scolding from Merlin, Cai was finished. He rolled up the message and tied it to the bird's leg. The little hawk fixed Rhianna with a blue-eyed stare and gave a final screech. Then he took off and flew away over the treetops.

Rhianna watched him go with mixed feelings. "What did he say?" she asked, pushing Alba into a canter.

"Never mind," Elphin said. "Let's hurry up and get Excalibur back before it gets dark. Which way now?"

Rhianna pointed to the mountains, and they set off again.

⚜

The track wound up and up, disappearing into shadow and then emerging into the light again. Rhianna wondered if she'd got the wrong mountain. But as the sun began to set, she saw the finger of rock standing against the red sky, just as she'd seen it through the shadrake's eyes. Thankfully, there was no sign of the shadrake or the red dragon it had been fighting.

Relief filled her. "That's it!" she said, pushing Alba into a gallop. "The lair's up there!"

"Wait for us, Rhia!" Elphin called behind her. "The dragon might be at home."

Cai's horse and Sandy got left behind on the steep slope, but Rhianna did not slow her pace. Evenstar raced at her side, a blur of white and mist. Her friend struggled with his bag as they galloped, trying to free his harp and ride at the same time.

As Alba clattered up the final rocks, she smiled grimly and drew the little dagger she'd stolen from the shadrake's treasure. She paused at the cave mouth.

It smells bad in there, her mare snorted.

"I know, my darling. You should have smelled the shadrake's lair."

I am glad I did not, Alba said. *You still stink of it.*

Rhianna grimaced as she headed the little

horse into the cave. She planned on riding straight in. But as the rock closed over her head, her heart began to thud and her breath came faster. She halted Alba and stared into the mountain, clutching her dagger in a suddenly sweaty fist as memories crowded in.

Chained in the dark... boulders falling all around...

Elphin stopped his horse beside her and put a sympathetic hand over hers. "Let me go in and get Excalibur," he whispered, dismounting. "Look after Evenstar for me."

Rhianna gripped her dagger tighter. "I'm not scared," she said.

He nodded. "I know you're not, but that little dagger's not going to be much use against a dragon. I've got my harp to protect me."

"But I'm the Pendragon! I should go.

The dragon won't hurt me."

"We can't be sure of that, Rhia. It stole your sword, remember. And don't forget Mordred's wearing the Crown now…"

While they argued in fierce whispers, Cai caught up. He was puffing almost as much as his horse, but he still had the Lance of Truth safely braced on his stirrup.

"Is the beast in there, Damsel Rhianna?" he called. "Do you want me to slay it for you?" His voice echoed around the rocks.

"Shh!" they hissed together.

Too late. The grey mare stumbled over the rocks at the entrance, sending stones sliding down into the lair with a loud, echoing clatter. Cai gripped the Lance tightly so it wouldn't follow. He stayed in his saddle, but the damage was done.

From inside the hill came a deep, grumbling roar. Sparks fizzed out of the cave, followed by a lick of flame. Alba danced sideways, shaking her mane. *The human boy woke the dragon*, she said.

Rhianna pulled herself together. "Get back!" she warned, as the red dragon that had stolen her sword rushed out of the shadows towards them.

It exploded into the sunset with a glitter of red scales and golden smoke.

"YOU WILL NOT STEAL MY EGGS!" it roared, swinging its great snout at them.

But one wing was torn, and the creature seemed unable to take off. It was limping from a nasty gash in one foreleg, leaving a trail of yellow blood. This gave them a chance to take cover behind the rocks.

"Eggs?" Cai whispered.

"The dragons must be breeding," Elphin whispered back. "Careful, Rhia – if they've got eggs in there, they'll protect their young before everything else."

She turned Alba to face the creature and took a deep breath. "I am Rhianna Pendragon!" she called. "You remember me, don't you? We don't want your eggs. I just want my sword back. If you let me have it, no one will hurt you, I promise."

The dragon shook its great head and belched flame at her.

"YOU DO NOT WEAR THE CROWN, PENDRAGON MAID. I DO NOT HAVE TO DO WHAT YOU SAY."

"Keep it talking, Rhia," Elphin whispered. "I'll go inside and find Excalibur." He shrugged his harp off his shoulder. Playing a gentle tune to work the invisibility magic they'd used to escape the Saxon camp last year, he disappeared into the shadows.

The dragon blinked at Rhianna and Cai in confusion. "WHERE HAS THE OTHER HUMAN GONE?"

"There are only two humans here," Rhianna said with a smile. Which was the truth, since Elphin was an Avalonian.

"I SAW THREE OF YOU."

The dragon limped around the finger of rock to peer behind it. Evenstar misted and reappeared down the hill where Sandy had fled, confusing it still further. It shook its big head and sank down to the ground with a groan.

"MY LEG HURTS. MY WING HURTS. THE OTHER PENDRAGON CALLS US TO FIGHT, BUT I CANNOT FLY."

Rhianna thought guiltily of how she'd sent the shadrake to its lair, and felt rather sorry for the red dragon. She glanced at the cave. Elphin had still not emerged. At least the dragon had not tried to roast them yet. But she felt so helpless without her sword, and it was getting dark down in the valley. Soon, they would not be able to find their way back down the mountain to the stone circle.

"Come on, Elphin, come on," she muttered, not wanting to disturb the dragon now it had settled.

Something black flew across the rapidly sinking sun. The dragon raised its head again, distracted. There had been two dragons in the ambush. Had the shadrake killed the other one? Or was it still inside? She looked at the lair again, her heart twisting in sudden fear for Elphin.

Cai gathered up his reins and pointed the Lance of Truth at the injured dragon. The magical weapon glittered in the last of the sunlight. "Go and get your sword, Damsel Rhianna," he said. "I'll keep an eye on the beast for you."

Gratefully, she dismounted and patted Alba. "Stay here with Cai," she whispered to the mare. "I'm going to see what's happened to Elphin."

She waited until the dragon looked up at the sky again, and made a dash for the cave. This time she did not let herself stop at the entrance, though her heart beat faster as the rock closed around her. She broke into a sweat under her armour and wondered what would happen if she took a wrong turn in the dark.

No, don't think of that.

She felt her way around a turn in the tunnel, which led down steeply. Her feet dragged slower with every step, but worry for her friend overcame her fear. Then her armour began to glimmer, showing her a dark pile of treasure reaching almost to the roof of the lair.

"Elphin?" she called. Was he digging through it?

At the sound of her voice, the glittering pile she'd thought was treasure stirred. A bright eye opened and blinked sleepily at her. She caught her breath and stumbled backwards, clutching her dagger.

The second dragon!

"I'm Rhianna Pendragon!" she said quickly. "I won't hurt you. I just want my sword back."

The dragon sighed and lifted its head. "THE DARK DRAGON HURT MY

MATE," it said. "BUT WE DID NOT LET IT STEAL OUR EGGS."

Rhianna felt bad again. She'd been responsible for bringing the shadrake here.

"The dark dragon didn't want your eggs. It was looking for my sword. If you let me have Excalibur back, you'll be safe and we'll leave you in peace."

Where had Elphin got to? Her heart began to pound again. Avalonians could not die, but they could be hurt in the world of men. If he'd been burned by the dragon's fiery breath, she didn't know what she would do.

She was about to ask the creature if it had seen him, when there was a rattle from the back of the cave and she heard the tinkle of her friend's harp. She breathed easier as the dragon lowered its head again and its eye closed.

"Move slowly, Rhia," Elphin whispered. "I can't play my harp and look for Excalibur at the same time. I can keep this one quiet, but I can't do much about its mate outside. Is Cai all right out there?"

"He's fine," Rhianna said, edging around the sleeping dragon. As she joined Elphin at the back of the cave, the sweat came again. The dragon's bulk looked exactly like the rocks that had blocked the tunnel in the shadrake's lair and trapped her inside…

"I'm here, Rhia," Elphin said softly, touching her arm.

She gave him a grateful smile as the memory faded.

She concentrated on looking for Excalibur, rather than thinking about the rock above her head. With Elphin's music filling the lair, it wasn't too bad. She wondered what they'd do if the sword lay beneath the eggs the dragon was sitting on.

Then her armour brightened again, and she saw Excalibur's white jewel poking out from under the dragon's tail. She breathed a bit easier, closed her left hand about the hilt and gave a firm pull. The jewel flared silver under her hand, and straightaway she felt stronger.

She grinned at Elphin. He grinned back.

Then they heard the flap of large wings followed by a yell from outside the cave. "Cai!" Rhianna said, running for the exit.

11

Druid Beacons

Fire blazed from every druid hill
Calling men afar, their blood to spill.
Over the sea Mordred's army did ride
While the living drowned on its ghostly tide.

They hurried out into the sunset to find the tops of the mountains on fire. A black-winged silhouette swooped through the orange smoke, terrifying the horses.

"The shadrake!" Rhianna gasped, gripping Excalibur tighter. "Where's Cai?"

She looked anxiously for Alba. The two mist

horses and Sandy shivered behind the finger of rock. She couldn't see Cai's grey mare with them and peered over the cliff edge, afraid she might see her friend's broken body far below.

Then Elphin pointed to the far side of the peak, where the boy bravely sat his horse in front of the injured red dragon, which pressed itself to the ground and hissed at its enemy. "Looks like that shadrake got more than it bargained for," he said with a smile.

Cai's horse reared as the creature swooped towards it. The squire lowered the Lance of Truth and set his heels into the grey's sides. He galloped across the plateau, yelling a challenge.

The human boy is brave, Alba said.

Rhianna shook her head. "He's going to get himself killed, you mean! What does he think he's trying to do?"

The shadrake had caught Cai's glittering lance in its talons, and the squire was lifted out of his saddle as he refused to let go. He clung determinedly to the shaft with both hands, his short legs kicking wildly in the air. The dragon flapped strongly, but could not get much height because of its awkward burden. The grey mare galloped off in panic.

"Hold on, Cai!" Rhianna shouted, scrambling over the rocks. She made a grab for the boy's dangling feet, but missed.

Cai shouted something at her. Elphin ran his fingers over his harp, but the music was drowned by the shadrake's roars. He shook his head. "Sorry, Rhia. My magic still doesn't work very well against creatures of Annwn."

Rhianna stood on the highest rock and raised Excalibur so that the blade flashed red in the last of the sun. "Let him go!" she ordered, wondering if her cousin was using the Crown to spirit-ride the beast.

The shadrake circled clumsily, then came back. The trailing lance rattled against the rocks. Cai still clung to it, looking terrified.

"Let go, Cai!" Rhianna yelled. "Jump! Don't worry about the Lance. I'll make the creature give it back."

This got the shadrake's attention. It made another clumsy turn and peered down at her. Its eyes glowed in respect.

"YOU SPIRIT-RODE ME."

"Yes," she said, shivering at the memory.

"LIKE THE OLD PENDRAGONS USED TO."

She smiled. "That's right. Let my friend go."

The shadrake circled in confusion. "THE

OTHER PENDRAGON SAYS I MUST BRING HIM THE GLITTERING SPEAR AND THE SHINING SWORD."

"The other Pendragon is not here," Rhianna pointed out. "Is he calling you? He'll be angry if you don't go to him right away. And my friend's fond of his food – it'll be hard work carrying him across the sea. And if you drop the lance in the water the other Pendragon won't be able to find it again."

"THAT IS TRUE."

The creature opened its claw, and both the lance and Cai fell.

Too late, Rhianna realised she should have told the dragon to land first. The shadrake circled once more, spooking their remaining horses. Then it gave a final shriek and flapped off into the dusk.

Elphin and Rhianna raced over to Cai, who lay in a crumpled heap at the base of the rocky finger. Elphin reached for his harp. But as they approached, the squire scrambled to his feet and gave them a shaky grin.

"Worried you that time, didn't I?" he said.

"Cai!" Rhianna scowled at him. "You could have been killed! Why didn't you let go of the Lance?"

"Because that shadrake was trying to steal it, of course! Besides, Merlin told me the knight who carries the Lance of Truth can't die. So I had to hold on to it, didn't I? Otherwise the beast would've iced me, for sure."

"You mightn't be able to die when you're carrying it, but you could still have fallen and broken your neck!" Rhianna said. "Look at Mordred. He's not dead, but he's missing a hand and has a crippled leg. What good would my champion be, if he can't fight duels for me? And now you've lost your horse."

"Well I wasn't hurt, was I? And we've got Sandy back, so I can easily ride him again until we find the mare. My boots just got a bit singed when the beast flew over the beacon, that's all." Cai looked at her feet in their filthy rags and grinned again. "At least I've still *got* boots."

Rhianna grimaced at the reminder, then realised what else Cai had said. *When the beast flew over that beacon.* She looked at the fiery sky in horror. "Those are the druid beacons, aren't they?" she said. "If my mother's lit them to call for help, Mordred must already be across the Summer Sea!"

Cai nodded. "They go all the way across the water to Camelot," he said in awe. "I've never seen them all lit up before."

"Then we've no time to waste. Is the Lance of Truth all right?"

"It's one of the four Lights, remember?" Cai said with another grin. Then he sobered. "I would've killed that dragon for you, Damsel Rhianna, if my silly horse hadn't galloped off. Sandy's not scared of dragons. Do you want me to kill the other one?"

She frowned at the red dragon, which they had all forgotten in the excitement. It crouched at the entrance to its lair, watching them warily. Elphin played a gentle chord on his harp. The dragon stretched out its torn wing with a sigh and lowered its snout to the rock.

"No," she said, still feeling sorry for the creature. "It's not the dragons' fault that Mordred sent them to ambush us and steal my sword. Whoever wears the Crown of Dreams controls the dragons, so when we get it back we should be safe enough. Besides, its mate is sitting on eggs in there. I don't think it'll follow us... will you?" she asked the red dragon.

"OUR CHILDREN ARE MORE IMPORTANT TO US THAN HUMAN BATTLES," it said. Then its eyes closed and it began to snore gently, letting out puffs of smoke.

The dragon dreams of eggs, Alba snorted. *It is silly. Apples are much nicer.*

"Half of Dragonland will able to see those beacons," Rhianna said, her stomach twisting with fresh anxiety as she mounted Alba. "We've got to get back to the stone circle. I just hope the knights haven't tried going back by road."

"They wouldn't leave us behind, Damsel Rhia," Cai said. "They'll come, don't worry."

"That depends if they can read what you wrote," she said. "Are you sure you explained Elphin's going to open the spiral path to take everyone to Camelot using the stone circles so we can catch up with Mordred?"

The boy bit his lip again. "Sort of… at least, I expect they'll guess the magic path will be quicker. You said not to write a song about it, Damsel Rhianna."

"You did, Rhia," Elphin said with a smile. The night breeze lifted his curls and the flames lit half his face, making him look very Avalonian.

"It isn't funny!" she snapped, tired and sore now that the action was over. "It's all right for you. Mordred's never going to take an army of ghosts through the mists to Avalon and steal your father's throne! I bet you don't even care what happens to poor Arianrhod, do you? Don't you understand? I left my father's secret jewel with her, the one Mordred needs to destroy before he can rule Camelot, and she's locked in the dungeon so she can't even *run away*."

Her voice had risen. The red dragon's tail twitched, and its talons clutched at invisible prey.

The dragon dreams of eating horses, Alba said nervously. *Maybe we should go now?*

"Then we'd better hurry," Elphin said, echoing her mare. Calmly, he bagged his harp, helped Cai up on Sandy, and mounted Evenstar. "Don't worry, Rhia, we'll stop him."

Rhianna sheathed Excalibur, suddenly very weary. At least the fiery sky would light their path.

They rode back to the stone circle in silence. Seeing no sign of the knights at the shadowy stones, she tried to persuade Elphin to open the spiral path immediately and take them back to Camelot. But he shook his head.

"We should at least give them until morning, Rhia. They mightn't be able to follow Merlin in the dark. If we go back through the stones, and the knights do come here looking for us, then they'll be even longer getting back. Besides, I'm not sure I can open the path without Merlin's help. This circle's very old, and there are echoes of dark magic here. I don't want to send everyone to Annwn by mistake, and anyway, you need some sleep before you face Mordred again."

She knew he was right, but it didn't make the waiting any easier.

Cai found firewood and whistled happily as he made a camp for them inside the stones. He'd brought along a burning brand from the last beacon, and used it to light their fire. He gave Elphin a proud stare. "See? We knights of Camelot can do without magic tricks," he said.

The Avalonian boy smiled. "What do you think lit that beacon?"

"Er… magic tricks?"

"Exactly. That's why Merlin went with the hawks, isn't it? So how would you have lit it on your own?"

"I'm not on my own, am I?" Cai said.

There seemed no answer to that. Rhianna leaned back against a stone and unwrapped the rags from her feet. She touched her blisters and winced. She hoped the knights would bring some spare boots with them, because she didn't fancy fighting Mordred and his army of ghosts with nothing on her feet. She bit her lip and started to wrap them back up again.

A six-fingered hand stopped her. The first trill from Elphin's harp made her stiffen. But then her feet stopped hurting and she felt warmer.

"Better?" her friend whispered.

She smiled at him. "I didn't mean to snap at you, earlier."

"It's all right. You're worried about Arianrhod. I am, too. We don't know very much about her, do we? I know you smashed the dark mirror, but what if she's still helping Mordred? Do you think she'll give him the jewel?"

Rhianna frowned. "No. At least, not willingly."

Cai gave up trying to tie his cloak between the stones to make a shelter and joined them. "I know I called her a witch's maid before, but Arianrhod's on our side. She kept Excalibur hidden back in the summer, remember – when we swapped the swords so I could take the wrong one to Mordred. If she were working for the dark knight, she wouldn't have done that."

Elphin nodded. "I agree, but there's something strange about Arianrhod. I sensed it when I played my harp for her the day she tried to take your pendant. I think she might have more to do with your quest than we realised. Why did King Arthur really take that jewel out of the crown, do you think?"

"To stop Mordred using it if he got his hands on it, of course. Merlin told us the Crown's magic wouldn't work properly without all the jewels in place..." Her voice trailed off.

"Mordred's already using the Crown. He's summoned an army out of Annwn. You wore it yourself, and you used it to spirit-ride the shadrake when it was trying to kill us, so the magic obviously works well enough. No Rhia, I think your father and Merlin were trying to hide a secret, and it must be a secret too dangerous for any man to know."

"Something about the Grail..." Rhianna whispered.

Elphin looked sharply at her. "What makes you say that?"

She shook her head. "Just something my father's ghost said. He couldn't remember what, though. If this secret's supposed to be too dangerous for men to know, then why did he tell my mother to give the jewel to me?"

Cai grinned. "And since when are you a man, Damsel Rhianna?" he teased. "Even if you dress like one."

Her cheeks went hot, and Elphin smiled. "Your father must have made his jewel into a pendant, something only a damsel would wear, to keep it out of Mordred's hands," he said gently. "If it does contain the secret of the Grail of Stars, then we have to stop Mordred getting hold of it at all costs. King Arthur told Guinevere to give it to you, but he obviously wasn't too worried if Arianrhod saw it. I wish we knew why she was left outside Camelot as a baby."

"I know!" Cai blurted out. "Maybe

Arianrhod's half fairy, and that's why Elphin likes her so much…" He flushed at the Avalonian boy's purple look. "Sorry, Damsel Rhianna, but mothers often abandon their babies if they think a fairy fathered them – didn't you see anything in the Crown about her?"

She tried to remember if she'd learned anything about her friend. But she'd worn the Crown for such a short time, and she'd been too busy spirit-riding the shadrake to look for any other secrets.

"What I'd really like to know is who *Mordred's* father is," Cai continued. "Don't suppose you saw that when you wore the crown, Damsel Rhianna? Lady Morgan would never tell anyone."

Elphin raised an eyebrow. "Did you see who Mordred's father was, Rhia?"

Rhianna shook her head, distracted.

"Maybe you can find out when you wear the crown again?" Cai said cheerfully. "The squires took a bet on it, and we'd all like to know."

"Why don't you ask Mordred when you see him?" Rhianna said, her head spinning. "I've got more important things to think about now than squires' gossip."

The two boys glanced at each other. "We should all get some sleep if we're planning on fighting a battle against Prince Mordred and his army of the dead of tomorrow," Elphin said, and strummed his harp softly to make the fire burn brighter.

Rhianna rolled herself into her cloak with a sigh. Had she made a very big mistake, leaving her father's jewel with Arianrhod?

❈

She woke from a nightmare of being buried in the shadrake's lair to a chill, damp dawn. Their fire had gone out. Smoke from the druid beacons hung above the trees, and she couldn't see her friends. She snatched out Excalibur and leaped to her feet.

"Shh!" Elphin said, jumping down from one of the mossy stones. "Someone's coming."

Her friend's Avalonian ears were sharper than hers. Very faintly now, she heard the drumming of horses' hooves. But even accounting for the distance and the gloom, she could only see a small party, not the proud troop of knights who had ridden out from Camelot.

"Where's Cai?" she said.

"Gone to meet them." Elphin pointed to

the young knight cantering through the trees on Sandy to meet the riders, his lance glittering in the dawn light.

"Why didn't you wake me?" Rhianna said, snatching up Alba's bridle.

"Because you needed your sleep, and they're coming here anyway." He put a hand over hers and stared at her with his violet eyes. "And I wanted to get you alone for a moment."

Her skin prickled. She wondered if he was going to kiss her again, as he had at the midsummer feast.

But he touched the spiral pathfinder he wore around his neck and said, "I don't know how Arianrhod fits in yet, but I've been thinking about that jewel of your father's, and I'm wondering if it might contain directions to the Grail Castle."

Rhianna frowned. "But my father never found the Grail of Stars!" she protested.

"So everyone thinks. The knights failed in their quest to bring it back to Camelot. According to our songs, the only ones who saw it are dead now. But we know both the Sword and the Crown can be used to contact the dead. Maybe the knights who saw the Grail told Arthur their secrets after they died? That jewel might well contain the only knowledge we have of how to find the fourth Light."

She stared at him. "And Mordred's going to destroy it!" she whispered. Then she remembered how she'd mentioned her father's secrets in the shadrake's lair. "Unless he decides to use it first..." She couldn't decide which would be worse – her cousin wiping King Arthur's name from history, or finding the Grail of Stars before she did.

"We mustn't let him get hold of it, either way." Elphin said, squeezing her hand. "I'll help you all I can. But I have to warn you, Rhia, my magic won't be much good against an army of Annwn. I can help you fight Mordred and his bloodbeards, but only the Lights have any power over ghosts."

She pulled herself together. "Then Cai and I will have to deal with them between us, won't we? The ghosts aren't important. It's Mordred we have to stop… oh, why don't they hurry *up*? What's Cai doing now?"

She watched the knights gather around the squire, their horses snorting in the cold air. The grey mare was with them, looking exhausted, her reins broken. The boy seemed to be telling them everything that had happened since they split up, pointing up the mountain towards the red dragons' lair and waving his lance about excitedly. Finally, he pointed to the stone circle. The knights turned their horses and galloped towards her and Elphin.

Rhianna hurried to saddle Alba, aware that Elphin's violet gaze still lingered on her. But she hardly had time to think about what he had said. Her head spun with images of her cousin seated on the throne of Camelot wearing the Crown... Annwn's ghostly warriors bringing the Grail of Stars to him... Arianrhod clutching the black jewel saying, "I'll guard it with my life"...

Alba nudged her. *Evenstar's rider is worried*, her mare reported.

"He's not the only one," Rhianna muttered. "We have to get back to Camelot before

Mordred gets hold of that jewel!"

She led the mare across the circle in such a hurry, her mist horse almost trampled the merlin as it glided low across the circle to perch on the nearest stone. It had a fat mouse trapped in one claw, which it proceeded to swallow in three bites.

"That's better," sighed the druid's spirit. "Can you actually hear me now, Rhianna Pendragon? Or have those dragons scrambled your brain?"

"Merlin!" she said in relief. "Where are the rest of the knights?"

"Never mind. We haven't much time, so just shut up and listen for once. This circle has gaps in it because of the fallen stones, which makes it dangerous because you could easily lose your way in the mists. When Elphin opens the spiral path, I'm going to have to stay on this side to make sure Morgan Le Fay doesn't lure you all off the path into Annwn. Remember what I told you about the Crown of Dreams? If Mordred's got into Camelot and restored Arthur's jewel to the crown, you'll have to be very careful. Best thing you can do is delay him until I get there, and—"

"Rhianna Pendragon!" boomed a voice. A big horse cantered across and stopped nose-to-nose with Alba. Sir Bors dropped out of the saddle and crushed her in one of his unexpected hugs. "Don't you ever, *ever* go off on your own in enemy territory like that again!" He held her at arm's length and looked her up and down. "What happened to your boots?"

Rhianna started to laugh. She couldn't help it. The laughing turned into tears, and she sniffed them back hurriedly. All the knights were watching, as well as her friends and the merlin.

"Never mind my boots," she said, raising her chin. She rested her hand on Excalibur's hilt. "What happened to Sir Lancelot and the rest of the knights? I sent a message telling you all to come to the circle. The roads are flooded."

Sir Bors glanced at Sir Bedivere. He coughed awkwardly. "We couldn't read half of it," he admitted. "Lancelot saw the druid beacons lit up last night, and all he could think of was the queen, so we said we'd stay and look for you so he could ride back to Camelot and help her. Don't worry, Damsel Rhianna. They got across the river before it burst its banks. They'll ride as fast as they can."

"We'll be faster." She swung into Alba's

saddle and glanced at Elphin. He clutched his spiral pathfinder and nodded.

The knights, who had all done this before, took their places behind the Avalonian boy as he led the way around the circle. The mist horses' manes shone silver in the gloom. Cai's lance glittered. Excalibur's jewel glowed.

The merlin finished scraping mouse fur off its beak and called, "I'll fly back the long way and meet you at Camelot. Don't do anything stupid until I get there, Rhianna Pendragon!"

The little hawk spread its wings and began to fly around the circle in the opposite direction, making Rhianna dizzy every time it flashed overhead. The back of her neck prickled as the air inside the circle began to sparkle. Dragonland with its damp hills and its mossy stones disappeared.

For a few breaths, she was alone with only her mist horse's sweet scent and the magic of the spiral path around her. She patted Alba's neck. "Let's hope it's not raining at Camelot," she whispered to the mare, and drew Excalibur in case they had to fight immediately.

Then the mists parted, and she saw her friends and Sir Bedivere and the other knights turning their horses in confusion. Alba snorted and picked up her hooves in surprise.

It is very wet!

Rhianna's heart sank. They'd emerged in the stone circle where they'd picnicked in the summer. But instead of being on a dry hill an easy half day's ride to Camelot, the stones were surrounded by water gleaming under a stormy green sky for as far as they could see.

"Go back, quick!" Elphin turned Evenstar,

his mist horse's silver-shod hooves skimming the surface, while the other horses splashed and floundered behind him. But as the last knight appeared from the stones, the path closed with a final sparkle.

Elphin clutched his spiral and stared warily at the water. "I'm sorry, Rhia," he said. "Merlin's closed the path. We're trapped."

Dark Knight
at the Gates

Mordred sat his black stallion outside the gates of Camelot and gazed up at the battlements. He had dreamed of this moment all year. Admittedly, in his dreams the gates had stood open to welcome him, rather than being shut in his face. But that was a small point, easily put right now that he wore the Crown of Dreams.

He adjusted the crown on his head and threw back his cloak so that his armour shone in the dawn. He had tied the reins around the stump of his right wrist so that he could grip his war-axe in his good hand, and before leaving the boats, he'd washed his hair in the floodwater that by now had hopefully drowned Arthur's knights.

"How do I look?" he asked his bloodbeard captain.

"Very kinglike, Master," the man said.

Mordred smiled. "Have you got the girl's things?"

The bloodbeard lifted a pair of small deerskin boots and the battered Pendragon shield they'd taken from his cousin when they'd captured her in Dragonland.

"Good. Then let's wake Camelot's lazy squires!"

Mordred waved his axe. At his signal, one of the bloodbeards blew a loud blast on a horn. The warriors of Annwn, surrounding the hill below the walls, howled eagerly and rattled their ghostly shields with pale swords. Those warriors that were out of reach of the Crown's magic stayed invisible, of course. But an eerie green mist rose out of the flooded ditches, making the sound even more frightening.

At Mordred's side, Uther Pendragon's ghost bared his teeth at the castle and shook his rusty sword. "Guinevere!" he roared. "Where are your manners, girl? Open up! I want to see the lass my son took to his bed, the one who couldn't give him an heir."

"Get lost, traitor!" A lanky dark-haired squire scowled down at them from the battlements and raised his bow. The weapon trembled as he took aim, and his arrow glanced off Mordred's axe to fall limply on the path.

Mordred laughed. "Is that the best you can do?"

The boy yelled something else, and a line of young heads appeared along the wall beside him. More arrows rained down – mostly way off target, but one went through Uther's ghostly body to land shivering in the grass. His green horse snorted and danced sideways.

"Not bad," Uther commented. "If I'd still been alive, that arrow might have killed me."

"Maybe it'd be wise to move back a bit, M-master?" said the bloodbeard captain, sheltering under the Pendragon shield.

"Oh, stop cowering like a scared damsel!" Mordred snapped. "Nothing can harm me while I wear the Crown of Dreams – watch!"

He rode his stallion forward until its nose touched the huge wooden gates, and spread his arms wide. He stared up at the young defenders. "Well, go on then!" he called. "Be heroes! Kill me… if you can."

The dark-haired squire had a good try. His next arrow flew straight for Mordred's exposed throat.

Mordred closed his eyes and concentrated on the jewel of Annwn. It warmed against his forehead, and there was a bright green flash on the other side of his eyelids. It made his head throb. But when he opened his eyes again, the arrow lay in two pieces in the mud, and the boy was staring at his broken bowstring in confusion. The other squires quickly ducked back behind their battlements.

Mordred laughed. "See? None of your

weapons can harm me while I wear the Pendragon crown. What's your name, boy?"

"Gareth," the lad said, sullen now.

"Well Gareth, as you know I'm Mordred Pendragon. King Arthur's daughter lies dead and buried in Dragonland. That means the throne of Camelot is mine now, since I'm the only one left alive with Pendragon blood. That's how it works, isn't it old man?"

He glanced at Uther and smiled at his grandfather's nod.

"Now then, Gareth. Run and fetch the queen for me, and maybe I'll let you be my squire when I'm king. You're not a bad shot with that bow of yours, considering. Better than that so-called champion my cousin brought with her to Dragonland. Fine lot of use he was, when we killed his princess."

The boy's gaze fell on the Pendragon shield in the captain's hand. He paled. "Princess Rhianna's dead…?"

"That's right. And all her knights and her little friends by now, too… just as you and your friends will be before tonight, if you don't hurry up and do what I say."

Gareth's head disappeared. The lad was gone such a long time, Mordred wondered if he would need to give the idiot squires another demonstration of his power. Using the crown to turn aside the arrow had already given him a splitting headache.

He closed his eyes with a scowl. But before he could call on the magic again, the gates creaked open. He tensed, half expecting more arrows. But his Aunt Guinevere had come to welcome him herself, still in her nightgown with her copper hair loose and flaming in the rising sun. She clutched a knight's cloak around her... one of Lancelot's, no doubt.

She took one look at the Pendragon shield and the boots dangling from the bloodbeard's hand, and gave a little scream of fury. A dagger flashed out from under the cloak, and she launched herself at Mordred.

"Murderer!" she shrieked.

He was so surprised, he didn't have time to raise his axe. He might have expected such behaviour from his cousin, but not from his Aunt Guinevere, whom he'd held captive all last winter and beaten the spirit out of – or so he thought. His bloodbeard captain was caught by equal surprise, unable to draw his sword because he still held Rhianna's boots and shield.

Uther's hand shot out in an attempt to catch the queen's wrist. The old man moved fast, though of course as a ghost he could not touch her, and her blade passed right through the dead warrior to strike at Mordred. But the magic of the Crown saved him again. The jewel flared green, and his aunt staggered backwards. The dagger spun from her fingers and disappeared into the nearest ditch. The queen collapsed before Mordred's horse, her bright hair spread out around her head like a fan.

A shocked hush fell.

Everyone stared at Mordred, waiting to see what he would do.

This was going even better than he'd hoped. He smiled and dismounted. Passing his axe to his bloodbeard, he limped across to Guinevere and knelt beside her.

He drew off his gauntlet with his teeth and laid his palm on her brow. She was still breathing – but that could be turned to his advantage.

"My poor aunt!" he said in a concerned tone. He looked around and spotted the dark-haired squire who had tried to kill him earlier hovering at the gates. "Don't just stand there, Gareth!" he snapped. "Find someone to carry the queen up to her bedchamber. Tell her maids to make up a fire to keep her warm. Oh, and while you're at it, send my mother's ex-maid down to me – the dark girl with the witch-mark on her cheek. She's still here, I understand."

The squires glanced uneasily at one another.

"She's in the dungeon," Gareth said eventually. "Is the queen…?"

"Dead? No, not yet. But the maid must attend me as soon as possible so we can get the formalities over with. Once I'm king, I'll be able to use the Crown's magic to heal Guinevere."

The squires whispered again. Nobody seemed to know what to do. Then two ancient knights came staggering out with a stretcher and gently lifted the queen on to it. They gave Mordred black looks as they staggered back inside with their burden.

They left the gates open. It wasn't exactly a royal welcome, but the squires reluctantly stood aside to allow him through.

"Good!" Mordred said, taking his horse's reins. Ordering Uther and his ghostly army to stay outside to guard the castle, he beckoned to his bloodbeards. "Let's go and see if Arthur's throne fits."

◁◦ 12 ◦▷

Ghost Warriors

Camelot stood against the flood,
Her walls surrounded by lakes of blood
And ditches filled with demons dread,
When a damsel rode back from the dead.

"Where's the road gone?" Cai said.

The knights blinked about them in despair, while their horses pawed at the flood. Poor little Sandy stood on the highest part of the hill with water up to his belly, snorting suspiciously at the swirling green weed.

"Crazy fairy boy must've brought us to the wrong stone circle," muttered Sir Agravaine.

"No." Sir Bors pointed to the familiar white towers, rising out of a green haze on the horizon. "Look, there's Camelot, right where it should be – except there's a dirty great lake between us and the queen. We'll just have to do some swimmin'! Make sure your packs are secure, tie your cloaks around your waists, and keep your swords out of the water. I don't like the look of that green stuff."

It smells bad, Alba agreed.

"Can the horses swim that far?" someone asked. "And what about the ponies? There might be currents."

"Mist horses don't need to swim," Rhianna reminded them.

But no one was listening to her. The knights were trying to decide whether the Roman road would be passable, and if they should wait for Sir Lancelot and his men before they challenged Mordred.

"We'll be stronger together," Sir Bors said. "If the road's passable, Lancelot shouldn't be long. Two days at most."

"We haven't got *two days*!" Rhianna stared in frustration at Camelot's towers – so near, and yet so far away. Was her cousin standing on the battlements right now, laughing at them? "Aren't you worried about what Mordred might be doing to your families?"

"Of course we're worried, Damsel Rhianna," Sir Bors said. "But if Mordred's already at Camelot, and I'm afraid it looks like he is, then a couple more days won't make much difference."

"It'll make all the difference!" Rhianna said. "You don't understand! If Mordred destroys my father's jewel and wears the Crown of Dreams at the Round Table, then we've *lost*. My father can never come back, because Mordred will be king of Camelot and will wipe King Arthur's name from history, and mine, and probably most of yours as well."

The knights muttered among themselves.

"Maybe the Saxons will help us?" Sir Agravaine suggested. "They've got boats. If we can reach one of their villages, we might be able to get word to Cynric."

"We haven't time to look for Saxons," Cai said, picking up his feet in alarm. "This water's getting deeper. If you don't make up your minds soon, we'll have to swim just to find the stones again. Elphin's got Merlin's pathfinder, hasn't he? Surely he can find a way through this by magic?"

The men looked at the Avalonian boy in hope. "Can you lead us along safe paths through this flood, lad?" Sir Bors asked.

Elphin clutched the druid spiral. His eyes whirled purple as the water began to lap at the stones, and Rhianna knew how brave he was being because no Avalonian could swim. "Cai's right, Rhia," he said. "My magic will be more use here. I have to stay and help the knights."

She thought of them all trotting in circles after Elphin to find a safe path through the flood and took a deep breath. "Then I'll ride across the flood and delay Mordred until you get there," she said.

Sir Bors shook his head. "Over my dead body! I promised your mother I'd not let you out of my sight. You've already been kidnapped by bloodbeards and buried alive in a dragon's lair. I'm not goin' to lose you within sight of Camelot. If you ride across that water, Rhianna Pendragon, I'm warning you now I'm swimmin' right after you if I have to hang on to your horse's tail the whole way across. You're not going alone."

"*I'll* go with her," Cai said, holding the Lance of Truth clear of the water. "I've got the second Light and I'm supposed to be her champion now."

The horses were beginning to roll their eyes and plunge about as the water touched their bellies. To Rhianna's surprise, the other knights seemed to think this was a good idea.

Sir Bors frowned. "Sandy can't gallop over water. Don't be silly, boy."

Cai's face fell.

"You can ride Evenstar, Cai," Elphin said, making the boy's face brighten again. "I'll ride Sandy to find a path for the knights. I'll look after him for you, don't worry."

"I only want to get my father's jewel from Arianrhod before Mordred does," Rhianna said. "I've got Excalibur back now. We'll stay out of Mordred's way until you arrive."

She could always use the time to find out if her mother knew anything about the secrets stored in Arthur's jewel.

Sir Bors gave in, and the boys quickly swapped mounts. Elphin held the Lance of Truth, while Cai squeezed himself into the mist horse's saddle. The Avalonian boy passed him the lance and whispered something into his horse's ear, then splashed through the water to rescue Sandy. Evenstar whinnied, and Alba snorted. It sounded suspiciously like the two mist horses were laughing at them, but Rhianna was too worried to smile.

Before the knights could change their minds, she set her heels to Alba's sides and headed the mare across the green flood towards Camelot. She heard Cai gasp as Evenstar leaped after her.

❈

They galloped through glittering spray, faster than any ordinary horse could go. At first Cai clung to Evenstar's mane with the Lance of Truth jammed under his arm, looking terrified. But as the water stayed safely under the mist horses' hooves, he relaxed. Rhianna cast an anxious glance over her shoulder, but Evenstar seemed to be behaving himself. She gave the squire an encouraging grin.

"This is great!" he yelled. "No wonder you keep these fairy horses to yourself."

"Just don't fall off," Rhianna warned. "Because I'm not stopping to fish you out."

Tell him not to tug on the reins like that, Alba said. *Evenstar won't run away with him.*

Rhianna passed this on. "And don't drop that lance!" she added.

Cai just nodded, having no breath left to reply.

They reached the Roman road, which still looked passable in places. They saw some soggy sheep standing on it up to their knees in water and bleating for help. All the lower ground was flooded. The river that ran past Camelot looked more like a sea.

She wondered if the flood reached through the mists between worlds, and if it had flooded Avalon, too. What about the crystal caverns, where her father's body lay waiting for her to bring him the four Lights so he could return to the world of men? She had a horrible vision of swimming through crystal tunnels filled with water, the air in her lungs running out before she found the way to his sleeping body...

"Damsel Rhianna!" Cai called, interrupting her dark thoughts. "Look! Isn't that the Saxons?"

She realised they'd reached the bridge leading to Camelot. Or where the bridge should have been. Ahead of them, Camelot's hill rose out of the green water. She breathed a sigh of relief. She'd been afraid they might find the castle underwater, too. But then, of course, Mordred would have no throne to sit on –

even her cousin wasn't *that* stupid.

She could see no sign of Mordred or his bloodbeards. But an unnatural green mist hung above the flooded ditches, and Cai was right – Saxons in soggy furs were trying to reach the castle, led by a huge man with yellow braids and a golden torque around his neck.

Rhianna's heart lifted in recognition. "It's Chief Cynric! Let's find out what's going on."

"Careful, Damsel Rhia," Cai warned. "Don't forget those sneaky Saxons used to fight on Mordred's side."

"They signed a peace treaty with me," she said, drawing Excalibur. "They'll let us through, don't worry."

Cai bit his lip and readied the Lance of Truth. They rode up the hill side by side to join the men.

As they approached the first ditch, both Excalibur and the Lance of Truth gleamed brighter. The white jewel under Rhianna's hand warmed, and her skin prickled. The air turned ice cold.

I do not like this mist, Alba said. *It smells bad.*

Rhianna realised that the ditch contained more than water. Shadows writhed and hissed in the bottom. As they got nearer, two ghostly warriors rose out of the ditch, grabbed a Saxon by the throat and dragged him down beneath the green mist. They heard a thrashing and growling, like dogs fighting over scraps. He screamed horribly. A thin twist of darkness rose into the air like a torn rag, and howled as it vanished across the flood.

The other Saxons drew back, making signs against evil.

"Chief Cynric!" Rhianna called, ignoring the ghosts. "Have you seen Prince Mordred? Will you fight for me against him?"

The men whirled, swords raised. They stared at the two mist horses as if they had appeared from the sky. "Odin save us!" one muttered. "Caught between Mordred's devils and the Wild Hunt!"

"We're not the Wild Hunt," Rhianna said, fighting a giggle at the thought that he could mistake her and Cai for great heroes. "Don't you recognise me? Mordred stole my shield, but I've still got Excalibur."

"Princess Rhianna…?" The big chief strode across and stared at her in disbelief. He reached for her foot and warily touched the flesh showing between the rags. "She's alive!" he said.

"Hey, get your hands off her!" Cai said, jabbing the big man with the Lance of Truth until he stepped back. The other Saxons growled and jostled closer. Cai glared at them too, his lance ready to fight them all if need be.

Rhianna waved him away, a bit worried he might spear someone by accident. "It's all right, Cai," she said. "The treaty still stands... doesn't it, Chief Cynric?"

The Saxon chief stared wonderingly into her face. He looked at his men. Then he snatched her out of the saddle and swung her around in joy. "Mordred was lying. The Pendragon Princess is back from the dead!"

⁂

They moved out of the green mist, back to where the Saxons had made their camp. Over bowls of hot soup, they exchanged information.

It seemed the Saxons had seen the druid beacons on fire. Knowing this meant Camelot was in trouble and needed help, Cynric had recalled as many men as he could from the fields, crammed them into boats and rowed straight there. But many people and animals had drowned in the floods, and the villagers needed the Saxons' help to save their stranded families. By the time they'd arrived at Camelot, the dark knight and his men had already taken charge.

"Prince Mordred was already at the gates, Princess," the big man said. "I'm sorry. We did what we could, but he left his devils to defend the ditches. You saw what happened back there. The same thing happens every time we try to get near Camelot's walls. They're already dead, so we can't kill them. But they can tear our souls screaming from our bodies. It's impossible to get past even the first ditch, and Odin only knows how many more of the devils are hiding in the mist between here and the walls."

"But how did Mordred get inside?" Rhianna said, dismayed. She stared up at the dark knight's eagle banner flying from Camelot's highest tower. "Was he wearing the Crown? Did he use its magic?"

"Magic enough." Cynric grunted. "He had your dragon shield and your boots. He told everyone you were dead and showed them to the queen. Then there was this bright green flash, and she fainted, or worse… sorry, Princess, but they had to carry her back inside. Then the gates opened and he went in after her. We haven't seen him since."

Rhianna turned cold. If Mordred had

killed her mother, she'd never forgive herself for taking all the knights out of Camelot.

"That's because the guards will have dealt with the traitor," Cai said. "Especially if they think he killed Damsel Rhianna and hurt the queen!"

"I'm not so sure," Cynric said. "He had some of them bloodbeards with him. Not many, but enough to keep order inside if all Camelot's knights have gone off to Dragonland, as you say."

"If the guards don't kill him, the squires will!" Cai said fiercely. "They know the story of how he killed King Arthur. Gareth hates Mordred. He'll do it."

"They're probably dead by now, too," Cynric said glumly. "Poor brave lads."

Rhianna stared up at the closed gate and clenched her fists.

Mordred wanted to use the Crown of Dreams to wipe her father's name from history and take the throne. But if King Arthur had not existed, then neither would the court at Camelot, which he had built, so there would be no throne for him to take.

It was so crazy, she laughed.

The Saxons gave her sympathetic looks. "Poor maid," they muttered. "It's the shock, you know... Lost her father, and now maybe her mother too..."

"Where are the knights?" Chief Cynric asked Cai in a low tone. "Don't tell me they all drowned in the floods, like Mordred claims?"

"They'll be here, don't worry," Rhianna said, sobering. "They're just slow, as usual. They had to go the long way round."

Cai, who had been giving her a worried look,

grinned in relief. "Yeah, we rode right across the flood! It was brilliant fun. Elphin let me borrow his fairy horse, and he's riding Sandy. I hope he keeps him safe. At least it's a bit drier up here…" He frowned at the castle. "So how are we goin' to get inside, Damsel Rhianna? Do you want me to challenge Prince Mordred to a duel?"

"It's not a bad idea," Chief Cynric said, looking at Cai with more respect. "If you can lure the little rat out here, we might be able to grab him for you."

"I'll duel with the dark knight if you want me to, Damsel Rhianna!" Cai said bravely.

She smiled at his determined expression. "No – there isn't enough dry ground left for you to tilt on, anyway. I've got a better idea."

She took Chief Cynric aside and quickly explained what she wanted him to do.

He gave her a doubtful look.

"Are you sure you wouldn't rather wait for the knights, Princess?" he said. "It'd be safer."

"We haven't time to wait!" Rhianna said. "I've got to get my father's jewel from Arianrhod before Mordred destroys it, and this is the only way I can think of to get inside. Just don't tell Cai until we get up there. I don't think he's going to like it very much."

⟡

She could tell Cynric didn't like her plan, either, but he didn't have any better ideas. They made their preparations quickly. She remounted Alba and drew her sword. She waited until Cai joined her on Evenstar and gripped Excalibur more tightly. "*I call on the knightly spirits bound to this sword,*" she whispered. "*I need you to fight for me now!*"

The jewel on Excalibur's hilt brightened, and its blade glimmered. The air around her rippled as the spirits of the men who had been knighted by the sword and later killed in battle joined them. Maybe she did not need the living knights to win this battle. She saw the Lance of Truth glimmering too. Her friend's eyes shone with excitement.

"Straight up to the wall, fast as you can," she muttered to Cai. "No heroics."

The boy bit his lip. The Saxons had lent him a helmet, which was a bit big. When he nodded, it slipped down over his eyes.

"Can you see in that thing? she asked.

"Not much," he admitted.

"Probably just as well," Cynric muttered.

Rhianna straightened Cai's helmet, checked

the Saxons were ready and raised Excalibur in the air. "Charge!" she yelled.

As their horses approached the first ditch at full gallop, the mist rose to surround them with an icy chill. Like before, she glimpsed shadows writhing inside it. Frost formed on Alba's mane, and she wondered if they might freeze to death before they got past the ghostly warriors.

A long, shadowy arm reached up to grab her rein. The little mare misted to avoid it. Excalibur brightened and its hilt warmed under her hand. She brought the sword down on the arm and heard a wail of pain. The shadow fell apart before her eyes. The arm twisted out of the ditch, curled up like a burning leaf and vanished in a puff of smoke. The rest of the shadow rose after it into the sunlight and went howling back across the water towards Dragonland.

She looked anxiously at her sword and laughed. Excalibur's blade still gleamed brightly. At least she didn't have to worry about blooding the blade in *this* battle. Ghosts did not bleed.

Beside her, she saw Cai spear another ghostly warrior with the Lance of Truth. The same thing happened. When the magical weapon touched it, the shadow disintegrated, smoked in the sun and fled back to Annwn.

"We can kill them!" she shouted, swinging Excalibur more confidently at another ghost and taking off its head. "Four Lights stand against the dark, remember? And we've got two of the Lights!"

Out of the corner of her eye she saw the dead

knights in their shimmering armour battling the ghostly warriors of Annwn in the ditches. The strength of a hundred men filled her. She laughed and looked hopefully for her father's spirit, but could not see him. She practised using her sword in either hand, swapping it over each time they took a breather. Her blood sang, and she began to enjoy herself.

As they jumped the last ditch and galloped up the hill with the Saxons running behind, Mordred's ghostly warriors howled and launched a final attack. She glimpsed eyeless helms and maimed limbs, horrible scars and gaping wounds – the injuries that had killed these men and sent their souls to Annwn. Shadowy axes and swords swung at Alba and Evenstar, but glimmered through the two mist horses without harming them.

They had almost reached the walls when a tall, ghostly warrior wearing a winged helm stepped out of the shadows right in front of Rhianna. He had the bearing of a king, and his eyes gleamed with curiosity as they studied her.

"So, this is my infamous granddaughter," he growled. "You're brave enough to have fought your way through my army, that's for sure. But a girl cannot be the Pendragon. Let that young fool Mordred sit on the throne for a few years, and come with me back to Annwn where there is no pain. I'll make sure Lady Morgan looks after you."

"Never!" Rhianna yelled, swinging Excalibur at his head. What had he called her? Granddaughter? That meant he was part of the Pendragon family she'd come to the world of men to find... except he was dead now.

She wondered why he hadn't been taken to Avalon when he died, like King Arthur.

The ghostly warrior ducked. "That's no way to treat your old Grandpa Uther," he said with a chuckle, drawing his rusty sword and leaping towards her. "If you want a fight, I'll teach you a few tricks."

"I'll teach *you* some tricks, you mean!" Rhianna said, swapping Excalibur to her left hand and telling Alba to mist past him.

The ghost of Uther Pendragon spun round in confusion and squinted at her. While he was distracted, Cai swung the Lance of Truth at his ankles from behind. Uther tripped over the lance and stumbled backwards down the slope into the ditch, where Alba trampled him with her enchanted horseshoes, sending him after the other ghosts.

He forgot to look behind him, her mare said. *No wonder he is dead.*

Rhianna grinned. She heard a yell of warning from Cai, and swung Excalibur to behead another shadowy warrior whose long fingers had knotted around Chief Cynric's neck.

"Thanks," he grunted as the shadow wailed away. The Saxon chief grabbed Alba's tail and held on grimly as she pulled him out of the ditch.

Rhianna checked Cai was safe, and risked a look behind.

Now that their leader had gone, shadowy warriors were pouring out of the ditches behind them to flee back across the water in a green cloud. She saw ghostly horses with them, and felt a bit sad. Those poor horses had already carried their riders into Annwn once.

"Yah!" Cai said, shaking his lance after them. "Run, you cowards!"

The Saxons had re-formed in the shadow of the wall. They looked up grimly at Camelot's high battlements. Rhianna's arms ached from swinging her sword, and her hair crackled with frost. Despite the chill of Annwn in the ditches they had crossed, she was sweating under her armour. But they'd done it. Only two of Cynric's men had been lost to Uther's warriors as the Saxons fought their way up the hill.

Cai flopped over Evenstar's neck and rested the Lance of Truth on the ground with a sigh of relief. "I couldn't skewer Mordred if he stood right in front of me," he groaned. "So what's the plan, Damsel Rhianna? Are we goin' to climb the wall now? Because I think I need a rest first."

Rhianna sheathed Excalibur so that its magical light died. She checked that nobody was watching from above before she dismounted. She unbuckled her scabbard, strapped the sword to Alba's saddle and took the reins over the mare's head.

This was the part of her plan she did not like so much.

"Dismount," she told Cai. "Let Evenstar loose, and hide that lance somewhere."

The boy looked puzzled. "But what if I need it inside?"

"It'll be safer out here. So will Evenstar. He'll go and find Elphin and tell him where we are."

The boy looked as if he might argue. But then he slipped off the mist horse's back, scrambled into the nearest ditch and covered the Lance of Truth with fallen leaves.

Rhianna felt tempted to do the same with Excalibur. But the Sword of Light had to be inside the castle for her plan to work. She might not get out again so easily once she was through the gates.

Her sweat had cooled, making her feel shivery. While Cai was busy hiding the Lance, she kicked what remained of the rags off her feet and passed Alba's reins to Chief Cynric. "Don't mist, my darling," she whispered to the mare. "This man will make sure you get to your stable."

Why can you not take me to my stable? her mare snorted. *I am very sweaty. I need grooming.*

"I know you do, my darling. Cai will groom you. I have to see someone first."

She took a deep breath and held her hands

out towards the Saxons, wrists pressed together. "All right, tie me and make it look good. If Mordred thinks I'm your prisoner, he'll let you in."

13

Prince of Camelot

A traitor sits at the table round,
Prince of Camelot, as yet uncrowned.
But only the true and rightful heir
Shall rule the knights who gather there.

Last year, Rhianna had ridden into Camelot while her father's people cheered and showered her with white rose petals from the walls. This time, everyone watched in silence as Mordred's bloodbeard captain led her, bound and barefoot, across the courtyard. His other hand clutched Excalibur in its red scabbard.

The Saxons followed, scowling under their damp furs. In their midst, a small warrior wearing an oversized helmet cast worried glances at Rhianna.

She hung back a little on her leash. "Stop looking at me," she hissed. "You'll give us away."

The bloodbeard gave the leash a tug. She bruised her toes on the steps, but bit back her angry words. *Act meek*, she told herself. *Then he'll think you're beaten and will forget to be careful.*

She lowered her head so her hair hung in tangles across her face and limped a bit. The captain looked down at her bare feet and chuckled. "Missing your pretty boots, Princess?

You won't need them in the dungeon. No place to run down there."

Rhianna hoped he would take her straight down to the cells so she could talk to Arianrhod and find out what had happened to her father's jewel. But no such luck.

As they passed the dining hall, the bloodbeard turned to the Saxons and growled, "What are you lot still following me for? I think I can handle a barefoot damsel! Go and get drunk or something. No doubt Prince Mordred will reward you later for your treachery."

The small warrior in the oversized helmet hesitated. The others hustled him along with them into the dining hall, calling for mead. Two frightened maids ran in to serve them, casting Rhianna nervous glances on the way.

"That's right." The bloodbeard chuckled at

their shocked expressions. "Take a good look at your princess – not so proud now, is she? This is what happens to damsels who defy Prince Mordred. Tell all your friends."

Rhianna kept her head down so she wouldn't catch the girls' eyes. They were used to seeing her looking scruffy after she'd been sword training with the squires. It didn't matter what they thought, but she wished she could ask them about her mother. She hoped Mordred had not hurt the queen.

While the bloodbeard was distracted, she twisted her hands against the rope. Chief Cynric had only tied the knot loosely, and she had the other end clutched in her hand so it would come undone quickly. But she needed to pick her moment.

"Right – come on, you!" the bloodbeard

jerked her leash again. "I don't know how you got out of that dragon's lair. But now you're here, Prince Mordred will want to see you. Turns out we've got a small problem, so you might be of some use after all."

Rhianna's heart beat faster as they turned down the corridor leading to the Great Hall. A small problem? Maybe she wasn't too late to stop Mordred taking her father's throne.

The big double doors stood open. Her cousin sat in King Arthur's seat, slumped over the Round Table, his head resting on his arms and his dark curls shadowing his face. Sunlight poured through the hole in the roof, illuminating the Crown of Dreams, which encircled the central slot where Excalibur could be inserted into the stone. The crown flashed with colour, its large green jewel swirling with Annwn's shadows.

As she tried to see if her father's jewel had been restored to the Crown, Excalibur began to glow in response. Startled, the bloodbeard held the sword at arm's length. He cleared his throat. "Er, M-master...?"

Mordred looked up, squinting at the sun and all the flashing jewels. "What is it now?" he snapped. "I thought I told you not to disturb me in here—"

When he saw Rhianna, he snapped alert. His gaze flew to the sword in the bloodbeard's hand, then back to her. A slow smile spread across his face as he took in her bare feet, her tangled hair, and the rope binding her wrists.

"Well well, this is a surprise, cousin! You're proving remarkably difficult to kill." He jerked his head at the bloodbeard. "For Annwn's sake, give that sword to me before it swallows your soul, and get the girl away from it!"

The bloodbeard pushed Rhianna into the nearest chair and slid Excalibur in its scabbard across the table. But the Round Table was so big that the sword didn't slide all the way across. It came to rest touching the Crown of Dreams. The blue stone of the table began to hum, and both the Sword and Crown brightened as they touched.

Mordred pulled a face at the glowing crown and struggled to his feet. He limped around the table, holding on to the backs of the chairs for support.

As he came closer, Rhianna saw dark shadows under his eyes and a ring of weeping black blisters around his head. She winced, realising they had been made by the Crown of Dreams.

Mordred looked exhausted. "What are you staring at, cousin?" he snapped. "It's hard work wearing that Crown, you know. A damsel like you would never manage to control the magic. Be thankful I found it first."

"I wore it in Dragonland," she reminded him, unable to play the meek prisoner any longer. "And I used it to spirit-ride the shadrake! That's more than you can do, isn't it?"

Mordred laughed. "Still got a bit of fight left in her, I see. Leave us, and lock the doors behind you. My cousin and I have unfinished business."

"But Master…" the bloodbeard protested.

"Leave us, I say!" Mordred scowled and pressed his palm to his forehead, where the largest blister wept sticky fluid into his eyes. "She's unarmed and bound. I have the Crown and the Sword. What's she going to do? Kill me with her bare toes? I'll call if I need you."

Rhianna bent over her hands and started to work the knot loose. When the bloodbeard left, she'd get her chance. Once the doors were locked, the only way in or out of the hall would be through the roof hole, which was impossible without wings. It would be just her and Mordred and two of the Lights. But she'd need to move fast to get hold of them both before the dark knight did, and the knot had been pulled tighter on her way here.

The back of her neck prickled as footsteps passed behind her. Not yet... with her head down and her hair over her face, she couldn't see what her cousin was doing. She heard him mutter something to the bloodbeard.

Then the doors slammed behind her.

She tugged desperately at the rope, trying to pull her wrists free. But before she could get the last loop off, Mordred's hand twisted in her hair and pulled her head back.

"What are you up to, cousin?" he hissed into her ear.

Rhianna gave up on the knot and twisted out of his grip, leaving copper strands in his fist. She scrambled on to the table and dived for Excalibur with her bound hands. He cursed and grabbed her ankle, pulling her back. She sprawled facedown and blooded her nose on the stone, but managed to hook the scabbard towards her.

She awkwardly drew Excalibur two-handed in a shower of sparks. The sun coming through the roof hole dazzled her. Her blade flashed, reflecting the colours of the crown.

Mordred still gripped her ankle, surprisingly strong for a one-handed cripple. She kicked to free herself and swiped at him blindly with her sword.

He ducked and laughed. "Careful, cousin. Don't want to blood your blade, do you?"

"Neither do you, if it's *your* blood," Rhianna pointed out, swinging at him again.

But it was awkward, lying on her stomach with her ankle captive and her wrists still linked by the rope. Her arms ached from fighting her way up the hill, making her wish she hadn't shown off so much when dealing with the ghosts.

As she twisted round to use her teeth on the stubborn knot, her cousin grinned and raised his stump. There was a dark blur in the corner of her eye. Before she could react, a black gauntlet flew from his belt towards her. The gauntlet tugged her bonds tight again and clamped around her wrists to stop her freeing herself. Ice flowed up her arms – cold, so very cold. Her fingers went numb on Excalibur's hilt. Though she tried her best to hold on to it, the sword slid off the table and clattered to the floor.

The gauntlet, oozing its rotten flesh, did not let go, and she realised where she'd seen it before. It was Mordred's missing hand, which her father had chopped off during the battle at Camlann just before the dark knight killed him. His bloodbeards had been carrying it the first time she'd met them, when their captain had used it to torture Sir Bors in the Saxon camp. It contained the shadow magic of Annwn.

All the strength ran out of her. Mordred dragged her off the table and pushed her back into her chair. She tried to get up again but could not fight the shadow magic without her sword and sank back in despair, shivering.

He smiled down at her. "That's better," he said. "Amazing how powerful Annwn's magic can be when you know how to use it properly. I've learned a few tricks since we last met, thanks to my mother. And now I think it's time we had a little chat."

He picked up Excalibur and limped back to his seat. While Rhianna struggled to shake off the gauntlet and free her wrists, her cousin laid the sword before him on the table and put on the Crown of Dreams. The jewels on both Lights brightened. He smiled at her.

"I'm glad you got out of that cave, cousin.

I didn't like to think of you buried in there – it wasn't my idea. You can blame my mother for that. I expect you're the reason my shadrake failed to get hold of Excalibur and the Lance of Truth, as I told it to do, but no matter. The Sword is here now, and you're just in time to help me summon the knights of the Round Table so they can crown me the new King of Camelot."

"They'll never make *you* king!" Rhianna said, a flicker of hope returning. If Mordred summoned the knights, they would arrest him.

"Ah, but that's where you're wrong. I wear the Pendragon crown. They'll have no choice. But for some reason they won't come when I call. You know the secret of summoning them, don't you? My mother tells me Excalibur can summon the spirit of anyone who has ever sat at the Round Table, living or dead. Help me call the knights who knew me when I sat here as a prince of Camelot and Arthur's favourite, and I'll make sure the queen is looked after. I don't like killing family unnecessarily."

"You killed my father!" she reminded him through gritted teeth, seeing that he meant to get the dead knights to crown him while Sir Bors and the others were delayed by the flood. "You're a traitor, and I'd rather die than help you."

"That could be arranged, if you continue to be stubborn," Mordred said, frowning at her. "Though your friends will die first, slowly and painfully. Be sensible for once, cousin. I've destroyed your father's jewel and changed history. The little maid was ready to die because of you. So why not keep your remaining friends and family alive by helping me?"

Rhianna turned cold. She stopped trying to get the gauntlet off her wrists. "What have you done with Arianrhod?" she demanded. "If you've hurt her..."

Mordred's smile widened. "The girl's either very brave or very stupid. She told me she'd promised you she would guard that jewel with her life, and I hate to see anyone break a promise."

Rhianna leaped to her feet with a cry of rage, but still couldn't free her wrists from the dark fist. She eyed Excalibur's blade. Maybe she could distract Mordred long enough for her to run around the table and impale the gauntlet on the sword...

"*Courage, daughter,*" said a familiar voice.

"*Your maid is not dead.*"

"Father!" she gasped as King Arthur's ghost glimmered into view beside Mordred's seat. She was relieved to see him back from Dragonland and its gate to Annwn. But if history had been changed, how long would he be able to stay? "Be careful – Mordred's destroyed your jewel!"

Arthur frowned at the crown on the dark knight's head, then reached over his shoulder and tried to pick up Excalibur. His ghostly hands passed through the sword, but Excalibur's blade brightened and the crown flashed green.

Mordred winced and raised his hand to his head.

"*Take off my crown, traitor, and let my daughter go!*" Arthur commanded. "*Or I'll cut off your other hand when I return to the world of men.*"

Her cousin flinched. To Rhianna, her father looked more solid than he had in the shadrake's lair, but Mordred obviously couldn't see him as well as she could. He must have been able to hear him, though, because he laughed.

"You do that, uncle – *if* you return! I think we're going to have a long wait, though, before you can pick up your sword again... A very long wait, if you're relying on your daughter to find the Grail of Stars, which no knight has ever found and lived to tell the tale. So how can anyone expect a damsel to succeed?" He laughed again. "Especially alone, without her friends. Merlin won't escape the shadrake this time, and her fairy prince seems to have vanished off the face of the earth along with all your fine knights. No doubt the lad has seen sense and ridden back through the mists to Avalon by now."

Rhianna's heart thumped. "That's a lie! Elphin would never abandon me." But she couldn't help thinking of her friend leading the knights through Annwn's green flood, and the Lonely Tor that led to Avalon, only a day's ride away.

Seeing the doubt on her face, Mordred chuckled. "Are you so sure of that, cousin? I wear the Crown now. I can see through the shadrake's eyes, remember."

"Only if you can spirit-ride," Rhianna said. "Which you can't."

"Maybe I've learned how," Mordred snapped back. "Come, shadrake!" he called, raising his arms to the hole in the roof. "Come to your new Pendragon!"

A shadow passed across the sun. Her cousin looked up with a triumphant smile.

Rhianna's stomach tightened as huge wings blocked the light. But the dragon flapped on past. As Mordred squinted after it, a small, feathered missile dived through the hole above the Round Table and flew into the dark knight's upturned face, knocking the Crown askew.

"Merlin!" she gasped in relief.

Her cousin flung up his arms to protect his eyes, and the gauntlet's grip on her wrists loosened as he lost control of the shadow magic. She thumped it against the table, and the horrid thing dropped to the floor.

In a heartbeat, she had dragged off her remaining bonds, danced around the empty chairs, snatched up Excalibur and leaped on to the table. She thrust the blade into the slot that

Merlin had made for it long ago, and ghostly knights long dead shimmered into view all around the hall.

"Who summons us?" they breathed.

"I do!" Rhianna said quickly, before her cousin could speak. "I summon you to aid your king, Arthur Pendragon, guardian of the Round Table and rightful ruler of the world of men!"

The knights blinked at King Arthur's ghost. "Our king!" they whispered. "Our king has returned to Camelot… what is your command, sire?"

"*Throw the traitor Mordred out of here,*" King Arthur ordered. "*He has dared to wear my crown, but he will never be king of men while my spirit survives.*"

Mordred, meanwhile, staggered from his seat and stumbled around the hall, pursued by the screeching merlin. The ghosts crowded around him. He bumped into pillars and tripped over a chair as the crown slipped over his eyes. He backed into a corner, fending off the pale knights. "Get away from me," he growled. "*I'm* your Pendragon, not Arthur! Don't you recognise me? I'm Prince Mordred, son of the king's sister, Lady Morgan Le Fay, and I wear the Crown now! You have to obey *me*..."

Rhianna closed her eyes to concentrate on the sword's magic. "Sir Lancelot?" she called. "Sir Bors? Sir Bedivere? Can you hear me? It's Rhianna! I'm at the Round Table. Where are you?"

She held her breath. If Sir Bors and Sir Bedivere were still following Elphin through the floods, would they be able to hear her?

"Right outside!" boomed a voice at the door,

making her jump. "Hold on, Damsel Rhianna, we're coming."

The double doors burst open. Sir Lancelot and Sir Bors rushed in with the other knights who had ridden to Dragonland. Their armour dripped and they left wet footprints across the floor, but their weapons were dry. Cai stood behind them with his oversized Saxon helmet in his hand, grinning. Rhianna grinned back in relief. She left Excalibur in the table and jumped down, looking for Elphin.

She'd forgotten the dark fist.

As she jumped off the table, it flew up from the floor and seized Excalibur's hilt. The ghostly knights disappeared. In the shadows, Mordred jerked his right arm. The sword came out of the table with a shower of blue sparks and flashed straight for Rhianna's throat.

She staggered back against a pillar, where the sword pricked her chin. She swallowed in fear as something warm trickled down her neck.

Blood, she thought in horror. *Blood on Excalibur's blade.*

14

Shadow Magic

Two Lights shone bright in Camelot's hall
Where a dark knight sat among them all.
When Sword is set against the Crown
Then shall Mordred be struck down.

Everyone froze, staring at Rhianna and the blade the dark fist was holding to her throat. Despair filled her. Now she couldn't take Excalibur back to Avalon for her father. Even if she found all four Lights, she could not complete her quest.

Mordred struggled to his feet and struck the merlin a blow that sent the poor little hawk tumbling across the floor. He adjusted the crown, which had slipped over one eye, and spat out a feather. Before the knights could stop him, he limped towards Rhianna and grabbed her wrist, pulling her in front of him.

"Nobody touches me!" he said, twisting her left arm up behind her back. "Lay your weapons on the floor and let us walk out of here. And keep that crazy bird off me as well, or your princess joins my mother in Annwn. I mean it."

With the dark fist and the sword following her every move, Rhianna had no choice but to shuffle with her cousin towards the door. The merlin lay on the floor under the table where

Mordred had knocked him, wings spread and panting. She couldn't see Elphin. Where was he when they needed his magic? She heard the clash of swords in the corridors outside and wondered if the Saxons had changed sides yet again.

When she thought of how stupid she'd been to let go of Excalibur, she felt like crying. Then she got angry. This was her father's castle! Mordred had no right to threaten her inside Camelot.

"Don't worry about me," she choked out. "It's only shadow magic. Arrest him!"

The knights stared uncertainly at the dark fist holding the sword to her throat. Sir Lancelot took a step towards Mordred, who raised his right arm. The fist jumped sideways, knocking Lancelot's sword from his hand before returning swiftly to Rhianna's throat.

"I'm not bluffing!" he warned as Lancelot hugged his wounded wrist. "That's my right hand holding Excalibur, the one King Arthur chopped off at Camlann. It's been to Annwn and back, and I know how to use the shadow magic now."

"He's only trying to scare you!" Rhianna spluttered. "He won't kill me. He knows he'll never get out of here alive if he does."

The knights muttered angrily. But none of them dared approach the dark knight.

"That's better," Mordred said. "As you can see, my fist holds the Sword of Light. That means I command your knightly spirits now. So lay down your weapons and get down on your knees! And someone bring me my horse and the Lance of Truth. I know it's here somewhere, if the little champion is around. Don't make me look for it, or it'll be the worse for your princess."

The knights glanced at Rhianna again, but whoever held Excalibur controlled them. Slowly, one by one, they laid their swords on the mosaic floor and dropped to their knees. Cai cast her an apologetic look and hurried outside. Another squire went running towards the stables.

"Oh, for goodness' sake!" she said as Mordred dragged her past the kneeling knights, into the corridor that led to the courtyard. "I can't believe you're just going to let him walk out of here! He killed my father remember? Pick up your swords, you fools, and arrest the traitor!"

Sir Bedivere shook his head at her as they passed. "Your life is more important, Damsel Rhianna," he said. "Don't do anything rash.

We can't fight Mordred while he's got two of the Lights – the spirit magic is too strong. But Cynric's still outside. The Saxons aren't controlled by Excalibur's magic, don't worry."

"Those two-faced barbarians won't get in my way if they know what's good for them," Mordred growled as he hustled Rhianna down the corridor.

The fighting had stopped. Rhianna wondered who had won. She made it as difficult as she could for Mordred to drag her along, slowing him down as much as possible to give the Saxons time to get into position.

An out of breath Cai waited outside in the courtyard with the Lance of Truth. A small group of bloodbeards stood warily near the open gates with their horses. The shadrake crouched on the battlements, watching every movement with its red eyes. When he saw no sign of the Saxons, Mordred relaxed slightly and pushed her down the steps towards his men.

"Strap that lance to my horse's saddle and get down on your hands and knees," he ordered Cai. "I need a mounting block, and you'll do nicely."

"Don't do it, Cai!" Rhianna called. "Go and get Elphin. Tell him to bring his harp."

"Forget it," Mordred said with a laugh. "Avalonian magic doesn't work against the power of Annwn, as your fairy friend knows."

The squire stopped. His hands trembled as he aimed his lance at the dark knight. "*I'll* save you, Damsel Rhianna!" Teeth gritted in determination, he advanced towards Mordred. But since Rhianna had knighted Cai with Excalibur in the summer so that he could be her champion, he had the same problem as the other knights. With the sword held by the dark fist controlling his spirit, each step the boy took was slower than the last.

"Stop!" Mordred said in alarm, dragging Rhianna in front of him again.

Sweat broke out on Cai's brow. His face twisted in pain as he fought the magic, but he kept the Lance of Truth pointed at the dark knight and managed another step.

"I command you by the power of this Sword that controls your knightly spirit to stop!" Mordred yelled, a flicker of fear in his eyes. "You're the Pendragon's champion, aren't you? I hold Excalibur, which means you have to obey me now, not her! Do what I told you, or your princess dies, here and now."

Mordred's bloodbeards closed around their

prince and Rhianna. The knights were still weaponless, watching helplessly from the top of the steps.

Cai's shoulders slumped. He carried the lance over to the black stallion, mouthing "sorry" as he passed her. Was he really under Mordred's control, or only pretending to be? This was getting ridiculous.

She jerked her elbow into Mordred's stomach and stamped down hard on his lame foot with her heel. This might have had more effect if she'd been wearing her boots, but Mordred doubled over in pain and grunted as his crippled leg gave way.

Before he could recover, Rhianna ducked under Excalibur's wildly waving blade and grabbed the dark fist in both hands. It twisted in her grip and froze her hands, but she had anger on her side and prised the black fingers open one by one.

"Give me back my sword!" she yelled at the dark knight. "I'm not scared of you!"

"You should be," Mordred hissed as his captain helped him up. "You'll be sorry you did that, cousin. You can't fight magic."

"I've been fighting magic all my life," Rhianna growled back through gritted teeth. "What do you think I had to do growing up in Avalon?"

As soon as her fingers touched the white jewel on Excalibur's hilt, it flared brightly. Freed from Mordred's control, the knights shook their heads as if waking from a daze. They picked up their weapons and staggered down the steps into the courtyard to help Rhianna with her struggle against the dark fist.

Mordred retreated behind his bloodbeards and raised both arms to the sky. The green jewel at the front of the Crown glowed, and the shadrake swooped down from the battlements, its shadow darkening the sun.

He laughed. "See?" he called. "This crown gives me the power of the ancient Dragonlords! Keep the silly lance, if you want. I don't need the Light made by the hands of men. The Crown and the Sword should be enough for now to make people obey me. When I find the Grail, I'll be invincible!"

"You'll never find *that* without King Arthur's jewel, traitor!" Cai said scornfully, swinging the Lance of Truth at the dark knight.

Mordred scowled and turned to deal with the boy. Cai's lance sparkled through the air, in danger of skewering Rhianna. While her cousin was distracted, she wrenched Excalibur from the dark fist's grip and yelled at the knights to help Cai. Seeing that she had her sword back again and could look after herself, they at last tackled the bloodbeards.

Rhianna leaped towards the dark knight, meaning to put Excalibur to *his* throat and make him give her the Crown. But before anyone could touch him, her cousin fell to the ground and began to thrash about, clawing at his head as Arianrhod had done in the chapel before they had set out for Dragonland. Seeing they could not win, the surviving bloodbeards abandoned their prince and fled for the gates.

The knights gathered warily around Mordred, forming a ring of swords. Annwn's green jewel brightened still further, and the crown began to smoke. Mordred groaned and thrashed some more. Then his back arched, he gave a final spine-tingling scream, slammed to the ground and lay still. The Crown rolled from his head, and the dark knight's spirit twisted up over the wall and vanished.

As everyone stared at the dark knight's body, a wild shriek raised the hairs on Rhianna's neck. There came a rush of wings, and the shadrake swooped into the courtyard making everyone duck. The horses reared in terror and bolted out of the gate.

"I WILL TAKE THIS NOW, PENDRAGON," the creature's familiar voice boomed in her head.

Rhianna tightened her grip on Excalibur and threw herself over the Crown, yelling a warning to Cai to keep a good hold of the Lance. But the creature did not try to steal any of the Lights this time. Instead, its scaly claw grabbed Mordred's fist from where she'd cast it aside. Before anyone could react, the dragon had escaped over the wall with its prize.

She climbed to her feet, shaking. She eyed the Crown, wondering if she dared put it on and call the dragon back. No, she wasn't ready yet for another battle with magic. Let the dragon take its treasure – her cousin wouldn't be using his dark fist to torture anyone else now.

The knights had dropped to the ground when the shadrake attacked, covering their heads with their shields. They gave Rhianna a sheepish look and turned their attention back to Mordred. Her cousin lay rigid, his face still twisted with its final scream. Sir Bors poked him with his sword. The dark knight did not move.

"Is he dead?" she asked, her stomach doing strange things.

Sir Lancelot bent over the motionless body and put a finger to the dark knight's neck. He frowned, then looked up and nodded. The others relaxed slightly.

Sir Bedivere sighed. "The Crown must have killed him," he said. "There's an old druid's tale that says it will kill anybody who tries to take the throne unlawfully, but we've never seen its magic in action before."

"It killed Morgan Le Fay too," Rhianna told them, staring at Mordred. She still could not quite believe he was dead.

"Serves the traitor right!" Cai said fiercely, gripping the Lance of Truth. "I wish you'd let me kill him for you though, Damsel Rhianna. It don't seem real he was killed by magic like that. Is Excalibur all right?"

She examined Excalibur's blade, reminded of the blood. But with Mordred dead, maybe it wouldn't matter so much if she couldn't take her father his sword when she went back to Avalon? She could always leave Excalibur at Camelot with her mother until the king returned to claim his throne.

Chief Cynric arrived at the gates with a bloodbeard's head dangling from each hand. The big Saxon's axe dripped blood, and he was grinning. "Caught these two devils running off. Guess Prince Mordred won't miss them now. Do you need any more help, Princess?" he asked. "It's a bit wet outside still – you won't be having any jousts for a while, but we'll soon get the place cleaned up for you. What happened in here? Looks like the Wild Hunt hit it."

Rhianna looked around the courtyard with its scorch marks, dead bloodbeards and scattered weapons. "Magic did," she said with a grin.

While everyone argued about whether the Crown's magic had really killed the dark knight or he'd finally died of his old battle wounds from Camlann, Queen Guinevere appeared at the castle door. She wore a nightgown and her bright hair was still tousled from her pillow.

Her frantic gaze swept the courtyard. When it reached Rhianna, she let out a gasp of relief and rushed down the steps towards her. "Oh, my brave darling! Thank God. I could hardly believe it when I woke up and they said you were back. He told me you were *dead*! He had your shield and your boots…"

Rhianna's heart lifted in equal joy to see her mother recovered. She laughed. "I still had my armour, Mother. It's magic, remember?"

"I know, but I've been so worried." Guinevere held back her hug at the sight of the bloodstained sword in Rhianna's hand. "I see you've been fighting again... I hope that's Mordred's blood?"

The knights glanced at each other. Nobody corrected her.

"We've got King Arthur's crown back, my lady." Sir Lancelot picked up the Crown of Dreams and handed it to her. "It was in Dragonland with Mordred, just like Princess Rhianna said. I think there's a few jewels missing, but it still seems to work. It rejected Mordred when he tried to use it to claim the throne."

The queen gave a funny little smile as she took the crown. She touched the green jewel of Annwn, drew a deep breath and looked around the courtyard. "Where is the traitor?" she said in an icy voice. "Bring him to me."

Sir Lancelot rested a hand on her arm. "Prince Mordred is dead, my lady," he said.

The queen frowned. Then she spotted Mordred's body lying in the shadows and pushed the knights aside.

"Stay back, Your Majesty!" Sir Bors warned. "It might be a trick."

The queen stared down at the twisted body of the dark knight. "I think my champion has fought enough battles to know whether a man is dead or not," she said, making some of the knights chuckle. "Get the Saxons to build a pyre for him. We need to call a meeting of the Round Table to discuss what to do about the mess Mordred's floods have left behind.

Cai, go inside and fetch out that merlin before it soils the floor. Rhianna darling, you're excused. Go and have a bath and get changed. We'll talk about this later." She frowned at Excalibur's soiled blade. "You'd better get your squire to clean your sword as well. Your father would never leave it in that state after a battle."

Cai opened his mouth to protest. "I'm a knight now, not a squi—"

"Do you want to sit in another boring meeting?" Rhianna hissed, and he shut up again.

❧❧

While Cai rescued the panting merlin from under the Round Table, Rhianna kept her hand on Excalibur's hilt in case the druid wanted to say something to her. But the poor bird didn't even look capable of flying, let alone explaining how she was supposed to complete her quest now that Mordred had destroyed her father's jewel and blooded Excalibur.

"Where's Elphin?" she asked as the big doors boomed shut behind the knights and the guards took up their position outside, spears crossed.

"I think he's with Arianrhod," Cai mumbled, avoiding her eye.

Rhianna frowned. "We could have done with his help earlier. Mordred almost cut my throat out there." She touched the wound and shuddered, only now realising how close she'd come to death.

"I'm sure Elphin will play his harp for you when he's finished helping Arianrhod," Cai said more brightly. "Shall we go down to the dungeon and see if they're still there?"

They settled the injured merlin in the hawk mews on the way, and for once the druid made no protest about belonging in Rhianna's room instead. Her stomach tightened as they turned down the steps to the dungeon. The guards had gone, and all was silent below. She remembered how she'd left her friend a prisoner down here when they set out on their quest. If Mordred had hurt Arianrhod, she would never forgive herself.

The door to the cell stood open. Torches burned brightly inside, showing them the maid fast asleep on the bed. A new bruise showed on her cheek, but she was smiling as she dreamed. Elphin slumped on a stool at her bedside, his head bowed over his harp and his curls shadowing his face. He was sound asleep, too.

The sweet scent of Avalonian magic lingered in the air.

Rhianna saw blood on Elphin's fingers, and the angry words she'd been saving for him fled. She took the harp from his lap and gently set it on the floor.

Cai opened his mouth, "Huh! The lazy—"

"Shh!" she said. "He's exhausted. Don't wake him."

"Do you think there's anything left of King Arthur's jewel?" Cai said. "Elphin might be able to mend it, like he mended the Lance of Truth in the summer."

The same thought had occurred to Rhianna. She checked under the pillow, unsurprised to find no sign of the pendant. She cast a quick look around the cell and sighed. "We can ask Arianrhod what happened to it when she wakes up. The important thing is, Mordred didn't get hold of my father's secrets. My mother's got the Crown now – that'll keep Camelot safe until we get back. I've got something else to take care of first."

Cai brightened. "Lunch?" he said hopefully. "We missed it earlier."

In spite of her worries, she smiled. "No, I want to go up to the lake. I need to talk to Lady Nimue."

"But Damsel Rhianna, all the knights are in the meeting, and what about the floods? You can't go out riding so soon! What if there's trouble?"

"Mordred's dead. His ghost-warriors have gone back to Annwn, and the Saxons have taken care of his bloodbeards. The floods must have gone down if the knights got through.

And if you're worried about that promise I made my mother, not to go out riding without my armour, my sword, and at least one knight... well, I've got Excalibur and my armour, and I believe you told the queen you're not a squire any more."

Cai drew himself up and retrieved the Lance of Truth from the passage. "I'll ride Sandy," he said with a grin. "I want to make sure Elphin hasn't taught him any fairy tricks while he was off in those mists."

◄ 15 ►

Funeral

That night they built a funeral pyre
To burn the traitor in cleansing fire.
Arthur's jewel to the Crown restored
May bring back Camelot's rightful lord.

They paused just long enough to pick up
Rhianna's boots and Pendragon shield,
which Mordred had tossed into the armoury
once they'd served their purpose. Then they
saddled their horses and trotted out of the

gates into a pink and gold sunset.

Around the castle, floods reflected the luminous sky as far as they could see. Only the Lonely Tor was visible above the drifting mist that lingered over the water. The ditches, which had been full of howling ghosts on their way up to the castle, swarmed with Saxons clearing up after the battle.

Chief Cynric passed them, cheerfully dragging a dead bloodbeard by his feet. "Funeral pyre tonight, Princess!" he called.

Rhianna's stomach turned at the thought of watching her cousin's body burn. But Cai grinned and called back, "Make sure you build it high for Prince Mordred!"

"High as Camelot's towers!" the Saxons promised.

Sandy seemed none the worse for his

journey along the spiral path with Elphin. He seized the bit between his teeth and trotted boldly ahead towards the river.

Alba snorted. *The Saxon pony thinks he is a mist horse now. But he cannot gallop over water like me. Can we leave him behind again?*

"No, my darling," Rhianna said with a smile. "Not this time. I promised my mother."

A yell from Cai distracted her. Sandy came splashing back out of the water, shaking his mane.

"The bridge is still underwater, Damsel Rhianna!" Cai called. "We'd better go back to the castle. It'll be dark soon, anyway, and we don't want to miss Mordred's funeral. We can always go to the lake and look for the fish-lady tomorrow."

She frowned at the swollen river. She hadn't

considered they might not be able to get as far as the lake. Maybe she should have told Cai to ride Evenstar again.

"No," she said. "I've got to ask her what to do about Excalibur before anyone tries to clean it—"

"So! You have finally blooded your blade, Rhianna Pendragon," called a silvery voice from the water, making them both jump. "I thought it would only be a matter of time."

A large tail splashed, and the fish-lady from the lake surfaced in a swirl of green hair. Sandy shied, and Cai almost dropped the Lance of Truth into the water.

"Careful, young champion," Lady Nimue warned in an amused tone. "I might just decide to accept your offering this time."

Cai recovered his balance and scowled

at her. "I haven't finished with it yet," he said. "I need it to protect Damsel Rhianna."

"Protect her from what?" Nimue sat on the flooded bridge and splashed her tail in the river. The pink sunset glittered from her scales. "I see no enemies for you to fight out here. Prince Mordred's bloodbeards fled back across the Summer Sea with those devils he called out of Annwn. I drowned a few, and the Wild Hunt will take care of the rest when it gets here at midwinter. Let me see that sword." She held out a webbed hand.

"Stay back!" Cai said, pointing his lance at her. "What are you doing out of your lake, anyway? You can't just sit on that bridge drowning people, you know. We'll get a lot of visitors at Camelot now Prince Mordred's dead."

"Prince Mordred's dead?" Nimue paused, her turquoise eyes going distant. "Are you sure?"

"Of course we're sure!" Cai said. "Arthur's magic crown killed him, because he tried to kill Damsel Rhianna and make himself king of Camelot. We're burning his body tonight."

The fish-lady frowned. "Then make sure you burn all of it."

"We're not stupid. And you still haven't told us why you're not in your lake."

"Stop it Cai," Rhianna said. "It's obvious how she got here. She swam downriver with the flood." She took a deep breath and blurted out, "Lady Nimue, can you clean Excalibur like you did last time – after King Arthur blooded it in battle and his knights returned the sword to your lake? My father's ghost has vanished again, so I still need to take it back to Avalon for him."

The fish-lady's turquoise eyes narrowed. "Bring the sword here."

"Careful, Damsel Rhianna!" Cai warned.

But Rhianna was already trotting Alba across the swollen river to the flooded bridge. She held out Excalibur, keeping a firm grip on the hilt in case the fish-lady tried to take it to her underwater cavern again.

Nimue ran her webbed fingers along the blade and frowned. "This is your blood," she said.

"Yes…" Rhianna swallowed in memory. "But you cleaned it last time, after my father chopped off Mordred's hand in the battle – and that was Pendragon blood, too. Please try, Lady? Mordred's spirit isn't in the hilt this time, so it's only the blade that needs doing."

"I could try," Nimue agreed. "But you'll have to offer the sword to me properly, like your father told his knights to do when he was dying, so I can pass it on to someone else after it has been cleansed."

Rhianna frowned. "But I need Excalibur if I'm going to look for the Grail of Stars!" She tightened her fist possessively on the hilt. The thought of not finishing her quest, now she had come so far, made tears spring to her eyes.

"I can see you're not ready to give up your sword," Nimue said with a sigh. "There's no need for me to do anything. Just polish it as normal. The blood won't be a problem."

"But I thought you said I mustn't blood the blade if I wanted to take Excalibur to

Avalon?" Rhianna snatched back the sword in anger. "You mean all this time I've been trying to be careful, fighting dragons and bloodbeards and Mordred without getting blood on my sword, and now you're saying it doesn't matter?"

The fish-lady smiled. "It does matter. But only if it's someone else's blood. When your father used Excalibur to wound men, he lost power over them. That's how Mordred was able to kill him at Camlann, and I didn't want you falling into the same trap. You've done amazingly well. You have three of the Lights now. If Arthur's spirit is still not ready to return to his body, then you may indeed need to look for the fourth – but I must warn you, no one has ever managed to take the Grail of Stars into Avalon."

"Then I'll be the first!" Rhianna said, lifting her chin and meeting the fish-lady's luminous gaze.

Nimue smiled again. "I can see your spirit remains strong. Perhaps you are ready for the final stage of your quest... You remember the riddle I asked you when you first visited me in my lake? *What is the secret of the Crown of Dreams?*"

Rhianna frowned. "I already answered that one... the Jewel of Annwn. It's the big green one at the front that contains the secret of dragon riding and opens the gate of Annwn, so it's hardly a secret."

The fish-lady laughed. "You only answered part of it. Every jewel in that crown contains its own secrets, and every Pendragon adds new knowledge to it. If any of the stones are missing, its wearer can't see the whole picture. Your father's jewel was missing when you wore the Crown of Dreams in the shadrake's lair. If you are to find the Grail and complete your quest, you'll need to wear the crown with your father's jewel restored. But be warned, Rhianna Pendragon – you might not like what you see."

"Then Elphin was right! My father's jewel does contain the secret of the Grail of Stars! But Mordred told me he destroyed it… so how can I find the fourth Light now?"

"The jewel was not destroyed," Nimue said.

The fish-lady's eyes reflected the last of the light, and in their blue depths Rhianna saw a luminous swirl of a horse's mane.

Evenstar comes! Alba whinnied, pricking her ears.

Rhianna's heart leaped in hope. Elphin

came trotting down the hill with Arianrhod clinging to his waist. His dark hair tangled with the maid's, whose head rested on his shoulder.

A pang of jealousy made Rhianna's fingers tighten on her sword. Then relief that Arianrhod was recovered took over, and she waved. "Elphin! Over here!"

He trotted straight across the river to join them, his mist horse's enchanted shoes kicking up pink spray. "*Faha'ruh*, Nimue. *Faha'ruh*, Rhia," he said, checking her over for injury. His violet gaze paused at the scab on her throat, and his eyes darkened. Then he smiled. "What are you doing out here talking to the Lady of the Lake? You're supposed to be safe in Camelot."

"Safe?" She blinked at him in disbelief. "Didn't you hear how Mordred got hold of

Excalibur, made all the knights kneel to him, and nearly killed me? He got blood on the blade. I had to do something about it… where *were* you, Elphin?"

"Missed me, did you?" he said, teasing now.

"I missed your magic! I thought Lord Avallach sent you out from Avalon to look after me?"

"Mordred was wearing the Crown of Dreams and using the Jewel of Annwn. I couldn't challenge him. My magic doesn't work against Annwn's dark powers. But I'm here now, and Arianrhod's got something for you."

He smiled as his passenger reached into her dress and pulled out a familiar pendant. Except the stone was not black any more. In the dusk it glowed pink and red, picking up the colours of the sunset. It dangled from a new cord woven out of Evenstar's mane.

Rhianna stared at it, her heart beating faster. "My father's jewel!" she said.

She'd been so stupid. Why hadn't she realised her cousin would lie to her?

"I promised to keep it safe for you my lady, didn't I?" Arianrhod said with a little smile. "So now you can put it back into your crown and complete your quest. Then King Arthur will return to Camelot, and everything will be right again."

"And I'll be able to see my father's secrets," she said, turning to ask Nimue what other knowledge the crown contained.

But with a splash of her tail, the fish-lady was gone.

"But I don't understand," Rhianna said to Arianrhod, as they rode back up the hill to the castle. "However did you hide the jewel from Mordred?" She thought of their conversation in Dragonland. "Are you a witch?"

"Don't be silly, Rhia," Elphin said.

"But you're keeping secrets from me again, aren't you?" Rhianna continued, still annoyed that everyone seemed to think she needed protecting from the truth. "If you won't tell me how you were able to hide my father's jewel from the dark knight in a locked cell, I can always find myself another maid."

Arianrhod blinked.

"It's all right, she doesn't mean it," Elphin said, playing a quick ripple on his harp. "She's just fought an army of ghosts, saved Camelot from Mordred, and played another riddle game with Lady Nimue. She's tired."

Rhianna sighed as the music soothed her nerves. "Just tell me the truth," she said. "If you turn out to be Elphin's long lost sister, or you're a druid like Merlin and want to live in the body of a bird, I won't mind. I've already got one grumpy hawk. You can keep him company."

Arianrhod giggled. "I never keep secrets from you, Lady Rhia. I didn't know the truth myself, until I saw it in your father's jewel."

"You can see my father's secrets?" Rhianna's stomach fluttered.

"With Elphin's help," Arianrhod admitted. "I had a dream of my mother when Elphin played his harp for me in the dungeon."

"Arianrhod's mother was a Grail maiden,"

Elphin explained. "She had a baby, but she wasn't allowed to keep it in the Grail Castle because none of the maidens who look after the Grail of Stars are supposed to have children. So when her baby was born, she brought the child to King Arthur in secret. Your father promised Arianrhod's mother he'd look after her baby, and arranged for his knights to find Arianrhod abandoned on the hillside so nobody would think her special. It's all in the jewel… you'll be able to see for yourself when the Crown's mended."

Rhianna stared at Arianrhod with fresh eyes.

"Have you seen the Grail of Stars?" she asked, excited. "What does it look like? Do you know the way to this Grail Castle?"

"She was just a baby, Rhia," Elphin said gently.

The maid bit her lip. "I can't remember anything before I came to Camelot, my lady, I'm sorry. But hiding your pendant was easy enough. You remember how we fooled Mordred with the lookalike Excalibur in the summer? When Gareth warned me Prince Mordred was on his way down to see me, I simply hung a dark stone from my jewellery box on the chain around my neck and pretended it was the real one."

"But wasn't Mordred suspicious after the trick we played on him last time?" Cai interrupted. "He was pretty angry about that fake sword I took him at the North Wall."

"He ordered his bloodbeards to destroy all my other jewels, too," Arianrhod admitted, touching the bruise on her cheek. "They smashed them with their axes."

"So how did you hide the real one?" Rhianna insisted.

"I swallowed it," Arianrhod whispered. "I'm sorry, my lady, but it was all I could think of to keep it safe for you."

"We've been waiting for it to come out the other end," Elphin added, wrinkling his nose. "Good job I had my harp to help."

"Yeuch!" Rhianna held the jewel at arm's length and grinned.

❀

Later, they all stood around the funeral pyre as flames leaped into the starry sky. The night had turned frosty, but the Saxons had built the pyre so high that it warmed the whole courtyard.

It seemed everyone had come out to watch

Mordred's body burn. The knights guarded the pyre with crossed lances. Wrapped in a fur-lined cloak, the queen stood with Sir Lancelot. She held the Crown of Dreams on a purple cushion.

Rhianna could feel the heat of the fire on her cheeks from where she stood near the back of the crowd. Even so, she shivered as the dark knight's body began to smoke.

Elphin gave her a concerned look. "We can go back inside, if you're cold," he whispered. "No one will mind."

"No," Rhianna said, setting her jaw. "I want to make sure he's really dead this time."

She half expected her cousin to jump out of the fire and charge at her with his battleaxe in his hand, yelling curses. But the flames licked along his crippled leg and burned up his hair, and all that happened was the fingers of his remaining hand curled.

He killed my father, she reminded herself as the smell of roasting flesh reached them. *He betrayed his king and the Round Table. He deserved to die.* It wasn't as if they were burning him alive. So why did she feel this upset?

"He won't be coming back from that," Cai said in a satisfied tone.

"The shadrake took his fist," Rhianna reminded them, thinking uneasily of Lady Nimue's warning to make sure they burned all of him. "When the Crown's mended, I'll have to make the dragon bring that back so we can burn it, too."

"I think Damsel Rhianna's missing the dark knight already," Gareth said, giving Elphin a sly look. "I reckon she had a soft spot for Prince

Mordred – you lost a rival there, fairy boy."

"I did *not* have a soft spot for Mordred!" Rhianna drew Excalibur, making people at the back of the crowd look round and frown at them.

The merlin, which had been dozing on Cai's wrist, opened a sleepy eye. "Put Excalibur away, Rhianna Pendragon," he grumbled. "I'm not feeling well enough to talk to you yet. Mordred has quite a punch."

"Not any more, he doesn't," Rhianna said, pointing Excalibur at Gareth. "You take that back, Squire Gareth."

The boy took a step backwards and raised his hands. "Steady… I didn't mean it. I'm just glad Mordred's dead at last. I'd have killed him myself if he hadn't been wearing that magic crown. Who helped keep your precious jewel safe, anyway? Would have saved us all a lot of trouble if you'd told us what we were really meant to be guarding from the dark knight."

"You could have stopped Arianrhod swallowing it!" But she smiled, because Gareth could just as easily have betrayed her friend to Mordred. Realising she was being silly, she sheathed her sword and touched the pendant hanging around her neck. It glowed gold and orange in the firelight. *Her father's secrets.*

She could feel Arianrhod at her elbow, watching her. The maid had promised to take the Crown to the smith in the morning to get the jewel reset. Then Rhianna would be able to wear the third Light, and they could start looking for the Grail to bring her father back from Avalon. She hadn't seen King Arthur's ghost since Mordred had blooded Excalibur's blade at the Round Table. Did that mean it was no longer in the world of men?

"I'm sorry, Father," she whispered. "We're going to find the Grail soon, and then I'll return to Avalon for you, I promise—"

"*Did you think I'd miss my nephew's funeral?*" said an amused voice.

She caught her breath as her father's spirit strode through the crowd towards them. People turned to frown and blink at the ghost as it slipped past them. He looked more solid than Rhianna had ever seen him look before, and her heart leaped in hope. Maybe three Lights were enough to restore his soul to his body, after all?

He walked up to her and touched the scab at her throat, making her shiver. Then he closed his hand about the pendant. "*Give it to me, daughter,*" he whispered.

She stared at the ghost in amazement. The jewel did not drop through his fingers as she'd expected, but glowed bright gold in his strong fist.

Shivering a little, she let him lift the pendant over her head. Arianrhod started and peered uncertainly at the ghost. She blinked and dropped a quick curtsey. "Sire!" she breathed.

"King Arthur!" Cai yelled, pointing.

The merlin almost fell off his wrist. The bird opened one eye, looked hard at the ghost, and stuck its head back under its wing with a sigh. "That's all we need," Merlin grumbled. "A ghost everyone can see."

"King Arthur?" Gareth said, staring in disbelief at the ghost.

One by one, heads turned and people whispered in amazement. "King Arthur's back!"

they shouted. "Make way for the king!"

A path opened up through the crowd. As everyone watched in amazement, her father walked up to where Sir Lancelot stood with the queen, gently took the Crown of Dreams from Guinevere's cushion and pushed the missing jewel into place. It sparkled as he did so, lighting up his face. He held the crown aloft for all to see. Guinevere stared at the ghost and pressed a hand to her mouth. Sir Lancelot stiffened.

With great ceremony, King Arthur's ghost carried the Crown of Dreams back through the crowd to Rhianna. He smiled at her and settled the third Light gently on to her bright hair.

"*It's time you knew Camelot's secrets, daughter*," he said. "*Then you can complete your quest.*"

Dark Spirit

The smoke rising from the funeral pyre in Camelot's courtyard made Mordred feel sick. Through the shadrake's eyes, he caught a final glimpse of his blackened corpse in the flames. They were burning his body so he couldn't go back!

His triumph at finally managing the spirit transfer turned to fury. It might have a crippled leg and only one hand, but it was *his* body. He tried to make the dragon dive at the figures in the courtyard. But the stupid creature flapped higher into the night, ignoring him.

He ground his teeth, and was alarmed
when a cloud of ice appeared in front of
him. Then he felt the dragon's powerful
wings carrying him away from his enemies.
Mordred gave in. Let them burn his crippled
human body! He didn't need it any more.

As the shadrake carried his spirit over
the Summer Lands, he sneered at the silly
villagers herding their animals to higher
ground. The floods had caused more chaos
than he'd realised. Arthur's knights would
be kept busy cleaning up for weeks.

They flew across the Summer Sea, faster
than any boat, and the hills of Dragonland
flashed beneath him. It was like being on the
back of a runaway horse. Mordred felt some
of the same terror. Then he remembered
he didn't have his body any more – a spirit

couldn't fall off and get hurt, could it?
He relaxed a bit and began to enjoy the
ride. He wondered where the creature was
taking him.

They turned up a river, and he recognised
the valley leading to the shadrake's lair.
Of course. The waterfall gushed out of the
cliff just as he remembered, and the entrance
was still blocked by boulders. Uther and his
ghostly warriors waited outside, fully visible
to the dragon's eyes.

The shadrake showed no sign of slowing
down. It carried him straight through
the wall of roaring spray. He had another
moment of fear when he thought it might
crash into the cliff and kill them both.
Then the gate of Annwn appeared, and the
creature landed on a shadowy ledge outside.

His mother's spirit waited at the gate, glimmering green and very angry. The shadrake folded its wings and hissed ice at her. "Hello, mother," Mordred said, knowing he couldn't hide from the witch's gaze.

"What do you think you're doing?" she demanded.

"Spirit-riding the shadrake, of course," Mordred said, pride creeping into his voice. "If you'd taught me how to do this earlier, I might be sitting on the throne of Camelot by now."

His mother sighed. "You won't be sitting on anything ever again, if what Uther tells me is true. The girl has not only got hold of the Crown, but restored her father's jewel and will soon know everything about us. Foolish boy! Whatever possessed you to leave your body behind at Camelot? Didn't you realise Arthur's knights would burn it so you couldn't go back?"

"It wasn't much use to me, anyway," he muttered. "It could barely walk, let alone fight. That's why my cousin and her friends kept getting hold of the Lights. But things will be different now. Once I've learned how to ride this dragon properly, I'll go back and deal with her."

"And you think you can control that creature, do you?" the witch hissed.

Mordred remembered the terrifying flight across the sea and through the waterfall. "My cousin spirit-rode it, and she's only a damsel. How hard can it be? I just need a bit more practice, that's all."

"Ha!" his mother spat. "Not even Merlin

could control the shadrake. If not for me, the dragon would have carried your spirit straight into Annwn by now. But all is not lost. Part of your body still survives, thanks to Arthur. Show me."

At first he couldn't think what she meant. Then he remembered his dark fist, which the shadrake had snatched from the courtyard when his spirit jumped aboard. He concentrated, and the creature's claw reached into its pouch and dragged out the fist. It looked rather the worse for wear after his cousin had grappled with it for Excalibur, and it smelled terrible. Rotting flesh oozed out of the gauntlet.

His mother's lip curled as she examined it. "Not pretty, but it'll have to do. There should be enough of your body in that glove to keep

your spirit tethered in the world of men.
You can use shadow magic for the rest."

Mordred stared at her in alarm. "But
I don't want to be tethered—"

The witch muttered a spell under her
breath that made Mordred remember the
pain of dying. The shadrake beat its black
wings, and he felt something give his spirit
a kick. With a sickening lurch, he fell into
what remained of his old body.

Rotting flesh closed around him, crushing
him into a tiny dark space. He couldn't
breathe. He couldn't see. He could no longer
even hear the noise of the waterfall outside.

He started to panic. Then something
touched the gauntlet, and his mother
whispered, "Use the shadow magic, my
son. Make yourself beautiful again," and he

realised he could wriggle his fingers. The fingers of his *right hand,* the one Arthur had chopped off in the battle.

He stretched carefully, growing a right arm and then a shoulder. He added some muscles and grew a left arm to match. He spent some time on his face, determined not to make it too boyish or give it any scars. Then he grew two straight, strong legs. He stood up slowly and opened his eyes.

He felt fantastic. Only his right hand in its battered black gauntlet reminded him of his old, crippled body. But at least he had a right hand again. He imagined the fingers around Rhianna's throat and clenched them tightly. Green rot leaked out of the glove.

His mother looked him up and down with a critical eye, making him remember to add some clothes – a black tunic with his double-headed eagle embroidered in silver thread, a cloak, decent boots and a silver torque around his neck.

"Not bad," she said. "Seems you've learned something from that Crown, after all. Your cousin will hardly recognise you. Now, before you meet her again there are some things you need to know. No weapon except one of the Lights can harm your shadow body, so don't worry about Arthur's knights. Nor can fire, or anything else that harms flesh. But take good care of your right hand. That is still mortal. If it is destroyed, then your spirit will have nowhere else to go except to join me in Annwn for all eternity. This is your last chance in the world of men, my son. Don't waste it."

Mordred grinned. He looked down at the dizzying drop no sane man would attempt, spread his arms wide and sprang out through the waterfall. He landed on his feet, knee-deep in the river and shook his hair. The icy water barely bothered him. He laughed. He hadn't felt this good since the day he'd killed King Arthur.

"What are you all staring at?" he yelled at Uther's warriors, his voice echoing in the cliffs. "I am Mordred Pendragon back from the dead, and I have need of you."

"I hope you don't expect us to help you find the Grail of Stars?" Uther said, frowning. "Because that thing can kill spirits as well as bodies." The other ghosts muttered uneasily.

"No." Mordred smiled as he splashed to

the bank. "We'll let my cousin do the hard work this time. There's only one place she'll go when she finds it. We ride to Avalon."

ABOUT THE AUTHOR

Katherine Roberts' muse is a unicorn.
This is what he has to say about her...

My author has lived in King Arthur's country for most of her life. She went to Bath University, where she got a degree in Maths and learned to fly in a glider. Afterwards she worked with racehorses, until she found me in 1984 and wrote her first fantasy story. She won the Branford Boase Award in 2000 with her first book *Song Quest*, and has had me hard at work ever since, seeking out more magical stories for her to write.

www.katherineroberts.co.uk

 @AuthorKatherine   @PendragonGirl

With evil cousin Mordred dead, Rhianna and her friends set out to find the final magical Light – the elusive Grail of Stars – so they can harness its power to help return King Arthur's soul to his body.

But the quest soon proves more dangerous than ever before. When Mordred is sighted at the Lonely Tor and her best friend, the Avalonian prince Elphin, goes missing, Rhianna finds herself fighting for more than just the Grail.

Available now...
PENDRAGON LEGACY
⇥ BOOK 4 ⇤
GRAIL
OF
STARS

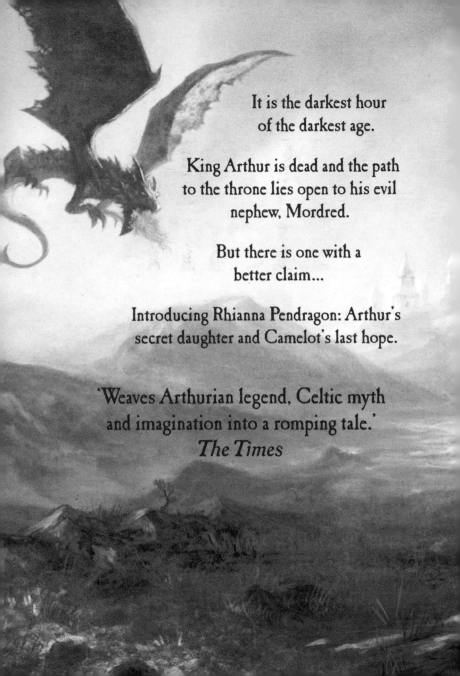

It is the darkest hour
of the darkest age.

King Arthur is dead and the path
to the throne lies open to his evil
nephew, Mordred.

But there is one with a
better claim...

Introducing Rhianna Pendragon: Arthur's
secret daughter and Camelot's last hope.

'Weaves Arthurian legend, Celtic myth
and imagination into a romping tale.'
The Times

Also available...

PENDRAGON LEGACY

⇒ BOOK 1 ⇐

SWORD
OF
LIGHT

The quest for Camelot's survival continues...

King Arthur's daughter Rhianna Pendragon has faced dark magic, ice-breathing dragons and mortal danger to win Excalibur, Arthur's sword. But Excalibur is just one of four magical Lights that Rhianna must find in order to restore her late father's soul to his body and bring him back to life. Now she must head into the northern wilds in search of the second Light, the Lance of Truth, before her evil cousin Mordred claims it.

But Mordred is also holding her mother Guinevere captive — can Rhianna stay true to her quest for the Lights and save the mother she's never known, before Mordred wreaks his terrible revenge?

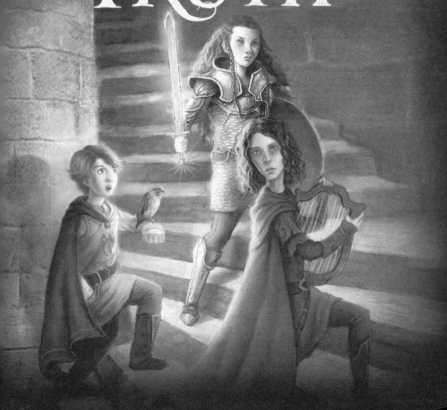